HIS TEXAS PRINCESS

PORT PROVIDENT: HURRICANE HOPE BOOK
THREE

KRISTEN ETHRIDGE

LAUREL LOCK PUBLISHING

CONTENTS

A NOTE FROM KRISTEN

Dear Reader,

I love fairy tales and a good tiara. I watch royal weddings. I drink tea from Harrod's out of commemorative mugs with pictures of princesses on them. I read splashy magazines with stories about charity events and comings-and-goings. I even had a set of Princess Diana paper dolls when I was a kid.

I may have a set of Duchess of Cambridge paper dolls now.

Okay, fine, and I have the entire British Royal Family Funko Pop set on a shelf in my study.

What can I say? Hey, everyone's got a hobby, right?

But what I love even more than crown jewels and palaces is when people I know find that hidden jewel inside themselves.

We are all made for a purpose. Some of us know it right away and plunge forward with no fear. Some of us know, but life finds a way to clip our wings. We flap and try to fly, but we struggle to soar. And then some of us need more time to search and discover who we truly are.

That's what I had in mind as I got to know the character of Anneliese. On the surface, she has everything. She's a princess of a small tropical island. She doesn't just have the tiara. She's got a beach too.

Inside, though, she's empty. She knows she's made for more. But she's boxed in. Rules of succession, paparazzi desperate to sell a story, and a brother who has a callous disregard for just about anything that doesn't directly benefit him—they're all working against Anneliese.

But one day, she's reading the newspaper. Something speaks to her. And she knows she has to make it happen. She learns to speak up. She learns to take risks.

She learns who she is.

And she learns what love really is.

I can't wait for you to meet Matt and Anneliese. I saw a lot of myself as I wrote this story, and I wonder if you'll see some of yourself too.

Port Provident isn't just a place, it's a place that's better because of you and how you connect with these stories. It's a community that you can be a part of every time you pick up one of these books. I think readers want more stories that are uplifting and make us think of the good in the world—because regardless of what the news tells us, it's out there. And that's why I created Port Provident—a town for all of us to visit for a sweet escape.

I'd like to invite you to join that reader community today. Just go to https://www.subscribepage.com/kristenethridgenewsletter. It's that easy!

One of my signature Sweet Escape Romances is Layla and Ridge's story, *A Place to Find Love*. Layla's spent her whole life searching for a greater meaning in her life. She comes to Port Provident running on fumes, but once she meets Ridge, she begins a journey that fills her with more than she ever hoped for—faith, family, and a place to find the love she's always longed for. I'll send you a copy just for joining my reader community, plus you'll be able to keep up with the latest on my books and Port Provident through regular emails and more reader bonuses.

Welcome to a Texas beachside town you can escape to anytime. I promise these stories will lift you up and leave you with a smile.

All the best,

Kristen

P.S... One of the best ways to get to know Port Provident even better is to get your *Passport to Port Provident*. It's a behind-the-scenes reader exclusive that's available when you join me on Facebook Messenger at www.facebook.com/kristenethridgebooks

www.kristenethridge.com
www.facebook.com/kristenethridgebooks
www.instagram.com/kristenethridge

PROLOGUE

"Well we sure dodged a bullet, but it looks like Texas took a direct hit." Crown Prince Federico de Cotriaro laid a newspaper in front of his sister Anneliese as they waited on their plates of *chilaquiles en mole* and *huevos fritas* for breakfast.

Every morning, the future king of the small Caribbean kingdom of San Petro looked through the basket of news briefs and papers that were brought to him. And every morning, the same people who brought her brother updates on what was happening in their world brought Princess Anneliese copies of glossy gossip magazines.

It was as if every sunrise served to remind her that her purpose in San Petro was to essentially have no purpose.

Hungrily, Anneliese picked up the paper her brother had brought to her attention.

"It says it made landfall in Port Provident, Texas."

Federico took a bite of honeydew melon. "Did it? I didn't look that closely."

Anneliese recognized the Texas town's name immediately. "Port Provident is Rosada's sister city. We should do something to help them."

"Anneliese, what could we possibly do for them that the American government won't do? Send them some papaya?" He stabbed at a thin slice of yellow fruit resting on the edge of his plate.

Long ago, she'd been taught to mask her emotions—so she couldn't roll her eyes at her brother, much as she wanted to. But she knew he was wrong. There were lots of things anyone could do to help someone in need.

Too bad Federico de Cotriaro was the neediest person in any room he happened to be in, Anneliese thought with a sigh.

"We could hold a clothing drive—I bet many people have lost everything. Or a food drive and send over non-perishable goods and bottled water. We're a small country, Federico, but our people are rich in heart."

"Anneliese, I love Americans. They come here and fill our hotels with tourists. They buy the rare Petroberyl emeralds we mine. They have turned our reefs into one of the premier vacation destinations in the world." Federico signaled for another cup of coffee. "But anything we could do for them would look like a pittance. I'm not going to the Americans looking like a pauper throwing his last dime in the collection plate."

Mariah, the breakfast attendant, placed Anneliese's plate in front of her. Anneliese looked at the jumble of chips and sauce covering half her plate. In her mind's eye, she imagined Port Provident, a city she'd never seen outside of photos, as a mixed-up mess as well.

As she started to eat her breakfast, Anneliese reached for the paper Federico had placed nearby. She began to skim the story. It unfolded much as she'd feared. Most of the island where the city was located had been submerged under a very high storm surge. Estimates said almost ninety percent of homes and businesses had sustained damage.

San Petro had been very blessed concerning hurricanes. Although their island sat in the crystal waters of the Caribbean, out from the border of Belize and Mexico, they'd only received glancing blows from the tropical cyclones that had periodically popped up and swirled during most of her lifetime. It made Anneliese's restlessness over the situation even stronger. They'd been so blessed—why was her brother so resistant to lending a helping hand to a place every school child in their capital city of Rosada knew about? They wrote letters to the school children of Port Provident. What could possibly make the Crown Prince of San Petro so dismissive?

Anneliese continued to read the story. Sandwiched in the middle was a quote from a David Long, the head of a group called Helping Hands Homes. He talked about how they were on-site and would be rebuilding homes for those in need at a greatly-reduced charge—and possibly even at no charge for those who had the highest levels of need.

"Why are you looking at your hands, Anneliese? Time for another manicure?" Her brother tried to make a joke, but as usual, fell flat.

"Not exactly." She rose from the table and tucked the newspaper under her arm. "Excuse me, Federico. I have some things I need to take care of this morning."

Federico leaned back in his chair and polished off his coffee. "Very well. Have a good day, *Hermana*. I will see you at dinner tonight."

Anneliese bobbed her head quickly in his direction, then headed down the hallway. She wound around the back corridor of the palace, where the staff offices were located. She knocked twice on the door to her private secretary but went in without waiting for a reply. She didn't want anyone to see her back here.

She was on a mission, and she didn't want any questions.

Or any roadblocks.

"Your Highness," Carlos Pampalón rose from his desk. "Am I late for an appointment? My diary doesn't show a meeting between us until this afternoon."

"Please, Carlos, have a seat. I know you haven't worked with me long, but I've told you, I don't have a whole lot of use for stuffy formality like Federico. If it's just you and me, you can call me Anneliese."

The older gentleman had served her family loyally for his entire career. "No, Your Royal Highness, I could not."

"Maybe Princess Anneliese?" She smiled, trying to make him comfortable with the idea of compromise.

Carlos smiled knowingly in return. "Maybe so, Princess Anneliese."

Anneliese placed the newspaper in front of her secretary. "Have you heard that Rosada's sister city, Port Provident, Texas, has been hit by a major hurricane?"

"I saw a bullet in the briefing document this morning."

"I want to help." She tapped the paragraph about the work Helping Hands Homes was doing. "I need you to get in touch with this David Long. Find out what I can do to help. Then get me a plane ticket to Texas at the beginning of next week. And whatever you do, don't tell Federico."

HIS TEXAS PRINCESS

1

———————

"*Y*ou'll be at the press conference at two, right?" David Long picked up a pre-packaged honey bun and a Styrofoam cup of lukewarm coffee off the folding table in the downstairs grab-and-go breakfast area that Porter's Gulfview Inn had set up for the contractors who were staying with them.

"Hadn't heard about a press conference, Dave. I've got a pretty full day on that house over in Alamo Court today." Matt McGregor looked over the options available, then decided on a personal-sized box of cereal and his own cup of lukewarm coffee. He'd take all the caffeine he could get this morning.

"Well, you're the director of the Helping Hands Homes Southern Region, and we're about as south as you can get without being in the Gulf of Mexico." Dave opened the cellophane surrounding the sticky pastry and paused to speak before taking a bite. "So I need you there. In fact, I'll make it easy for you. I'll have everyone come to your location instead. I'll see you a little before two."

Dave walked out the door before Matt could reply.

Matt drove from the motel to his job site with a frown on his face. He'd set some big goals for rehabilitating this World War II-era cottage in record time. Today was day one, and he needed to make sure his small crew stayed focused and got off to a fast start. Helping Hands Homes had set a goal to rehab or rebuild one hundred homes on Provident Island by Christmas.

It was an audacious goal, but Matt knew they could do it.

If they stayed focused.

And press conferences he didn't know anything about were nothing but a waste of time and a drain on focus.

"Morning, team." Matt parked his truck out front and was glad to see a small group of volunteers in green T-shirts alongside his regular work crew. "Come on over. Let's get today started."

The dozen or so people gathered in the front yard formed a semi-circle around Matt. He loved this part of the job. It reminded him of pre-game talks in football locker rooms—those magic moments when anything was possible if you believed you could win the game, no matter what.

Injuries had ended his football dreams, but his two years with Helping Hands Homes had given him the opportunity to be a part of the dreams of others every day by helping provide them with affordable, sustainable housing.

Plus, he was able to keep his hands dirty. He loved every minute of it.

"This is the Solares home. Mr. and Mrs. Solares live here, along with two kids and her mother, Mrs. Fernandez. As you can see, Hurricane Hope was brutal to the homes here in Alamo Court, most of which date from the late 1930s through the late 1940s. This particular house was built in 1946. So it's seen a lot of storms and a lot of history, and the Solares family assures me it's seen lots of love as well. They've already taken out everything they want. Our job today is to haul everything out here to the curb. I mean everything. We are taking this house down to the studs and rebuilding it completely. For those of you volunteering this week, we're glad to have you here. Don't be afraid to get your hands dirty."

Colin Baker, Matt's right-hand man on this job, took a step forward and then raised his hand. The regular crew followed his lead, then so did the volunteers.

"One-two-three…Helping Hands!" Everyone cheered. It was time to make the magic happen.

The morning passed swiftly, and Matt finally took a late break for lunch. He sat on a curb about two houses down from the Solares house and was polishing off the last bite of a red delicious apple—which he'd decided was very appropriately named—when a woman in jeans with a blonde ponytail came alongside him.

"Do you live here?" Her voice had the hint of a Spanish accent.

"I used to. I was born here." Matt stuffed the apple core in the brown paper bag that had carried the rest of his lunch. "Can I help you with something?"

"No, I was making sure that it would be okay to take some photos. I don't want to be disrespectful." She held up a sleek black DSLR camera.

Matt studied her for a moment. Just by looking at her, he could tell she didn't belong in Port Provident. She wore jeans and a T-shirt, but something about the fabric and fit didn't look like anything that could be bought here. Her hair was cut in delicate, long layers. She clearly didn't get it cut at some place in the mall.

"I guess as long as you're doing it with the right intentions, it would be fine. Are you a journalist?"

She shook her head. "Oh, no. Nothing like that. I'm hoping to share the photos with my school children."

So she was a teacher. That made sense. She had a quiet, calm demeanor. His sister was an elementary school teacher. Ellie had to cultivate patience by the bushel. Spending your whole day around kindergarteners required nothing less.

"Then I think you're perfectly fine." He stood up and pointed at the Solares house. "I've got to get back to work."

She reached in her bag and swapped out the lens on the camera. "Me too. Very nice to speak with you."

"You too." Matt tossed the small paper bag on top of a cardboard box full of trash from inside the house that had been hauled to the curb.

He couldn't keep himself from turning around and catching another glance at the blonde teacher. She was definitely the most pleasant thing he'd looked at since coming home to Port Provident to head up this project.

Regardless, he couldn't waste too much time on the view. He checked his watch. He had a stupid press conference in half an hour—and drywall to begin tearing out. As Matt walked back in the door of the bungalow, he knew he preferred the drywall.

In a different time and a different place, though…he might have preferred a little more conversation with the teacher.

Anneliese leaned in and snapped a photo of a cat scavenging in the bushes. It broke her heart a little, knowing that this poor thing probably had nowhere to go. Digging in her bag, she pulled out a packet of crackers and pulled out two. Walking slowly, she stretched out a hand with two crackers in front of her.

"Hi, kitty. Come here, precious *gatita*. I have a snack for you."

The cat fixed golden eyes on the crackers but didn't move.

"Oh, I understand. You've probably been through a lot. I'll leave these here for you and give you some privacy."

She tossed the crackers toward the cat, then took a few steps in retreat. The cat took two timid steps toward the crackers, then broke into a lightning-quick scamper. In seconds, the wafers had been spirited away to the hiding spot behind the thick green hedge near the front step of the small house.

A truck door slammed, and Anneliese jumped at the unexpected loud sound.

"Your Royal Highness! I didn't mean to keep you waiting." A man in work boots and jeans walked toward where Anneliese stood on the sidewalk.

She raised a finger to her lips. "*Sssh*. Please, not so loud."

"Oh, I'm very sorry Your Royal Highness." He lowered his voice to a normal speaking volume and Anneliese breathed a small sigh of relief. "We are thrilled to have you with us today."

"I'm glad to be here." She smiled warmly and put out her hand to shake, as she'd been trained her whole life to do.

"I'm David Long, President of Helping Hands Homes. I'm very pleased to meet you in person. We're very excited that you're interested in partnering with us." He took her hand in his own, then hesitated. "Am I supposed to bow or curtsey? I don't want to offend."

"No, please don't. I'm here as someone who wants to bring the well-wishes of the kingdom of San Petro and help the citizens of Port Provident. There's destruction everywhere. What's happened here is serious. Bowing and curtseying are trivial. There's no need for it here."

He gave her hand a simple shake instead of pomp and circumstance, then looked around. "Do you have anyone with you?"

"No, I've traveled alone on this trip."

Only Carlos had been given advance notice of her plans. She left a note for her brother and a message for her father's physicians and staff to relay to him—and then she turned off her cell phone. Only Carlos knew how to reach her. She needed to feel useful again, and she was not going to have her wings clipped by her brother's cynicism.

"There will be some reporters here—is it okay if they ask you some questions?"

Thankfully, she doubted the United States media had as much interest in her as certain nosy gossip papers in Latin America seemed to. She felt confident that she could use her title for some good here.

"Of course. I'll be happy to explain why I've come and partnered with your organization."

David handed her a manila folder with some papers in it. "My assistant, Debra, made you this packet. It tells what we have on your agenda for the next few weeks. Most of the time, I'll have you paired up with Matt McGregor, our director of operations for our Southern Region. He's originally from Port Provident, so I know he'll be a good resource for you."

Anneliese flipped through the folder's contents quickly. "This all looks fine. I see some of the TV trucks getting set up. Are we ready?"

"I think so." David gestured toward the end of the street. "We'll be standing in front of our current project, the Solares house. We are tearing it down to the studs because of mold and water damage, and then we'll be completely re-doing it on the inside."

The Solares house—so the man she talked to earlier must be a volunteer on today's project. It was good to see that others were moved like she was to come out and do something. "I'll follow your lead. Just let me know where to stand and signal me when it's my turn to speak."

"Sounds perfect."

She followed David down to the area that the Helping Hands Homes staff had arranged for the press conference. A number of TV cameras were trained on a small portable lectern adorned with a sign bearing the Helping Hands Homes logo. Anneliese sized up the contraption, grateful that the hurricane had already moved through because that narrow tabletop would probably blow away in a stiff breeze.

"Why don't you just stand right here to the left of me?"

Anneliese moved into position, and the TV crews circled close, flipping switches and focusing cameras.

"I'm missing Matt. Hold on. Be right back, everyone, and then we can start." David sprinted inside the small house behind them and came out with the man who'd been eating the apple earlier. The look on his face did not look nearly as amicable as when she'd first met him half an hour before.

David pointed at the assembled group and seemed to be urging the man to follow him. He did, slowly. He stood to the right side of David and folded his arms across his chest, obscuring the logo on his green T-shirt.

Anneliese watched him wipe his forehead with the back of his hand. She couldn't believe that he was going to stand there with that scowl on his face while the TV cameras were rolling. If she'd ever done that and been caught, it would have been splashed all over the media with some ridiculous headline about her being bored or angry… or some flimsy tie to the demise of her love life and how she must be devastated and showing it on her face.

Actually, it didn't matter what expression had been on her face for the last six months. The demise of her love life was all that anyone seemed to care to talk about.

That ended now. She was determined to prove her worth and her substance to a world who had the wrong impression.

"And so we are pleased to have with us, Her Royal Highness, Princess Anneliese of San Petro. The capital city of San Petro, Rosada, is a sister city to Port Provident. When Princess Anneliese reached out to our organization last week, wanting to know how she could help, I was thrilled to receive that phone call. As you know, it will take a lot of hard work and a lot of funds to bring the residents of Port Provident back into their homes. Princess Anneliese will play a significant role in helping us raise awareness, and for that, we're very thankful."

David beckoned for her to come over to the microphone. Anneliese took a deep breath and put on a smile. The time to begin rebuilding—not just Port Provident, but her own life—started right now.

Matt couldn't believe what had just happened in the last few minutes. He should have known that blonde wasn't a photo-happy teacher. He knew by looking at her that she was out of place.

Like several countries away out of place.

And then...when David handed him the paper with Princess Anneliese's schedule for the next two weeks and informing him that he was in charge of her while she was working with Helping Hands...

Babysitting a primadonna was not in his job description—and as soon as these TV cameras were out of the way, he was going to tell Dave so.

The steam coming out of his ears kept him from hearing anything Little Miss People's Princess had to say. The whole thing was ridiculous. He had 100 homes that he'd committed to restoring between now and Christmas. He needed volunteers who weren't afraid to break a sweat. He did not need pampered blondes from Caribbean islands who wouldn't know a hammer if it dropped on their professionally-manicured toes.

The assembled volunteers and workers gave a polite round of applause when the princess finished speaking. Dave looked back toward Matt, who decided to give his boss his best stone face. He was not a babysitter, and he was not a public speaker. There would be no remarks from him today.

Or ever.

Once the formal event wrapped up, two reporters stayed on the sidewalk, wanting to talk exclusively with the princess. Matt only cared to talk to Dave. And he would be doing all of the talking. Dave's crazy ideas had put Matt into a giant mess. His boss needed to be aware of that, in no uncertain terms.

"This is not over, Dave." Matt stalked off to stand underneath a large live oak in front of the Solares house.

"Matt—don't let her hear you acting like this."

"I don't care what she thinks of me. I care about the Solares family and if I'm doing a good job for them. I care about the citizens of Port Provident. I'm one of them. This is where I'm from. This is where generations of my family are from. I said we were going to restore one hundred homes by Christmas." He ran his hand through his hair. "That goal is personal to me, Dave. And I won't reach it if I'm babysitting your new best friend over there."

Dave looked him squarely in the eye. They'd worked together for years and had always been able to shoot straight with one another. But this—Matt regarded this as something close to betrayal. The job was about homes and families, not celebrities and royalty.

This wasn't the cover of *People Magazine*, for goodness' sake.

"If you want to achieve your goals, Matt, she'll be your new best friend too. You are almost one hundred thousand dollars short of the funds you need to pull off the bare minimum of your big personal goal. We're competing with telethons and established charities who are household names when it comes to disaster relief work. I don't have to tell you that this economic climate isn't exactly inspiring people to give money away. She's our ace in the hole—a pretty princess from a country that people love to daydream about. You can't raise the money on your own, but she can. I envision her getting the TV coverage and the magazine stories. And in every one of them, you can bet we'll put out our hands and ask for the money to make her dream—your dream—a reality. If you value your job and your goal, you'll get in line with this one, Matt."

Matt couldn't believe the tone his friend was taking with him. "Are you threatening me?"

"I don't have to. You won't achieve your goals for your hometown project if you don't get some more money in fast. That's not a threat. That's reality."

A reporter shouted Dave's name. He turned around and walked toward the white television satellite truck without another word.

Matt went inside the house and tried to get back on his game and back to work. He decided ripping out the water-logged cabinets in the kitchen would do the trick. The cabinets had been cheaply made, and all of the non-visible parts were particle board. They'd soaked up the stormwater and gradually loosened to the point where all Matt had to do was kick at the boards, and the cabinets fell apart.

Boom.

Boom.

Boom.

He'd been right. This felt satisfying, mind-clearing. He lost himself in the show of force and collapse of the cabinets until he heard a small voice behind him.

"Excuse me, sir? What should I do to help?"

Princess Perfect had walked into his sanctuary—the work zone. She didn't belong here any more than he belonged in a castle.

"There's nothing for you to do here. Why don't you go back wherever you're staying and do whatever it is Dave told you to do."

She dug in her messenger bag and pulled out a manila folder. "There's nothing on my schedule for this afternoon."

"Well, there's nothing here for you, either." He looked her over, taking in the slim-fit T-shirt and the midnight blue skinny jeans that ended in a pair of barely-broken-in work boots. Well, at least she'd tried to get that part right. He hoped she'd brought some bandages for her feet. Those things were bound to be rubbing blisters right this second.

"The people in your office told my secretary that you're short-handed and short on funds for this project. I've got two hands, and they're without anything to do right now. I'd like to help."

He couldn't deny that the tone of her Spanish-accented voice was sincere. She probably did want to help. But he could almost guarantee that she didn't know what that would mean in a case like this.

Matt leaned back against the refrigerator. He needed to get it out to the curb so he could finish the kitchen. In fact, he'd do that right now instead of continuing this conversation.

"Really, I can't be liable if you get hurt, Miss…Princess," he corrected, tugging at the appliance that had been without power for more than a week.

He made a space between the fridge and the wall, then jumped over part of the countertop and wedged himself in the cleared area and began to push. The wheels on the bottom of the fridge were stuck. Matt pushed harder.

Before he realized what was happening, the refrigerator toppled to the floor. The door popped open, and out came a smell that he imagined hadn't been sniffed since the Greeks talked about the rivers in Hades.

"Oh, my…that's…that's…just awful." Quickly, Matt wrapped the bend of his elbow tightly around his nose.

The princess looked at the mess, horrified. Her caramel eyes grew wide, and she shook her head. Without a word, she turned and walked out of the room.

All the satisfaction Matt had found in kicking and smashing cabinets evaporated. He'd now put himself behind because he was going to have to clean up this mess, and there was no telling how long it would take to do this if he couldn't breathe. He silently cursed himself out for shoving too hard on the fridge, trying to be a show-off to Her Royal Prissiness.

You certainly proved you know what you're doing here, McGregor.

Matt stepped over the frame of the lifeless fridge, trying to dodge the spilled contents. If he got any of this rotten filth on the bottoms of his boots, he knew he'd carry this moment with him forever. No chemical from any lab in the world would be strong enough to take the funk from his feet.

Matt kept looking downward as he tried to successfully navigated the food maze and as he took the last step, he walked right into something soft in his path.

"I thought we could clean this up," the princess said. "I pulled some boxes and trash bags and paper towels and such out of the supply truck. Do you think this will work?"

She held out a pair of disposable gloves that matched the ones she'd already put on. Matt took them, still stunned into silence by the fact that she'd come back.

"You'll probably want one of these, too." She handed him a blue bandana and then tied a red one securely around her own nose and mouth. "I don't know how much it will help, but something's better than nothing."

Arranging the supplies at her feet, she knelt on the floor. Molding grape jelly was leaking from a broken glass jar. Her knees landed right in the muck, but she didn't say a word. She just picked up ruined remnants of the Solares family's past and put them in the makeshift trash can she'd built from a cardboard box and some industrial strength black plastic bags.

Matt lowered himself to the floor beside her and picked up a package of hamburger meat that had now gone green.

"Thanks for letting me help," she said and kept on loading the boxes and bags until nothing remained on the floor.

2

—————

$\mathcal{A}$nneliese walked out the door behind the other workers and volunteers at the end of the workday. A bus came back to take the volunteers back to Houston. They all worked for an oil company named Dynacrude and were volunteering for the week together. She envied their camaraderie—and their transportation.

She'd walked from her hotel to the house earlier today, but now her work boots felt like lead, and she had blisters in places she hadn't even realized were part of her feet. There wasn't much sense in complaining about it now. There was a dusk-to-dawn curfew in effect in Port Provident, and if she didn't get moving, she'd find herself in violation of it before she made it back to Porter's Gulfview Inn.

About halfway down the block, she felt a shock of ice water slip through her veins. The neighborhood was silent—no one was living here right now—but the sound of a heavy, jogging footfall was coming behind her.

"Where are you going?"

Anneliese froze on the cracked sidewalk. Slowly she turned around. It was the man from the building project—Matt, she seemed to think they'd said his name was.

She tried to collect her wits about her so she could answer steadily. "Back to my hotel room."

"You can't just be walking around Port Provident by yourself." His voice was snappish, like one of the angry turtles who nested annually on the northern shore of San Petro.

"I don't have a license to drive."

"You don't need one. The state of Texas will accept your valid home country driver's license if you're visiting. Now, finding a rental car around here is probably a whole different matter."

Anneliese shook her head. "No, you misunderstood me. I don't have a license to drive. Anywhere. I've never learned how to drive."

The man's turned slightly, and he raised an eyebrow. "Never? You don't know how to drive?"

"I have a driver," she said matter-of-factly.

"Well you need one tonight then, too," he said. "You're not going to make it back to your room before curfew. Where are you staying?"

She pointed back in the direction of the Gulf of Mexico. "Porter's Gulfview Inn."

"Okay, that's where I'm staying too. Come on; you can ride in my truck." He waved a hand and turned back toward the house they'd been working on. She saw one beat-up white truck parked next to the curb.

"Wait."

He turned around, and that snappish turtle look was back on his face again. "What? We've got to go, or we'll get busted for breaking curfew. They take it pretty seriously around here, and I'd rather not have to call my great-aunt and get strings pulled to get me out of jail tonight."

She stuck out her hand. "Anneliese de Cotriaro. We haven't been formally introduced."

He looked at her hand with disbelief. "We're going to get arrested if we don't hurry and you want to make small talk?"

"I have diplomatic immunity." She smiled and put her hand out again, firmly. "Anneliese de Cotriaro. Pleased to meet you."

"Matt McGregor. Back at you." He put his hand out and gave hers one quick, tight shake. "Now, can we hop in the truck, please?"

"Certainly, Mr. McGregor. Thank you for the ride."

"It's Matt. Just Matt." His steps outpaced hers two-to-one. "Are you okay?"

"New shoes." She shifted her weight back to her heels. Hopefully, he didn't notice that she now had the general gait of a duck.

He unlocked the door to the truck and opened the passenger side for her to climb in. "Do I have to call you princess or anything?"

She settled in the front seat and buckled the seat belt as he hopped in the driver's side. "Well, no. I think I'd just prefer Anneliese. It seems more American."

Anneliese began giggling to herself at the thought of her brother's reaction if he'd heard her say that. Federico de Cotriaro would never stand for his sister wanting to be something as pedestrian as an American instead of playing up the fact that she was royalty.

"What are you laughing about?" Matt wound the truck through the deserted streets.

"My brother. He's kind of a snob."

"Let me guess. He's a prince?"

She nodded. "Indeed. The Crown Prince of San Petro."

"What exactly does that mean?" He slowed as they came to an intersection. The street light wasn't working, and Matt hesitated as he looked in all directions.

How could she best describe Federico? The good news is that he wasn't here to correct her assessment of him. She could speak freely if she chose to, but decided to keep it basic. No matter where in the world she happened to travel, discretion would always be the correct choice. But sometimes, she wished she was normal.

"It means he will inherit as king once our father dies."

"And what about you?"

They turned into the parking lot of the hotel. Matt shifted the gear to park and looked over at her.

"Nothing will change for me. I'll be expected to get married and do my duty."

She'd been reminded all too often this year that she'd fallen short of all those expectations.

"And that's it?" He turned off the ignition.

She frowned. Unfortunately, there wasn't much more to say about being a princess of San Petro, unless she wanted to let her tongue start wagging without discretion. And no matter how she felt about the gilded cage she'd been living in recently, she had too much royalty bred into her to not watch her words around strangers.

"Pretty much." She slipped two fingers behind the latch of the door and pulled. "Thank you for the ride, Mr. Mc—I mean, Matt. It was much quicker than walking."

She tried walking on her heels again through the parking lot, but it soon became clear that technique was not going to work, either.

Wistfully, she thought of her closet of Manolo Blahnik heels at home. No matter how high they towered or how skinny the heel was to balance on, never had any of her trusted designer shoes ever caused her feet pain like this.

Matt slung a backpack over his shoulder and caught up to her hobbling in about three steps.

"Why don't you come up to my room?"

Anneliese felt her shoulders snap backward. Had he seen the stories in the tabloids? "Well, I really don't..."

He cut her off. "Your feet. I've got some bandages and such that can help."

She looked down at the heavy leather boots. "My feet. Yes. That would be nice. Thank you."

"Have a seat. I need to look in my first aid kit and see what I can find." Matt left Anneliese sitting on the corner of the queen-sized bed in the rather plain hotel room. He wondered what she thought of a place like this. He was sure someone like her only stayed in penthouse suites and five-star luxury.

When he initially sized her up, he'd given her three days, tops, before she packed up her Italian designer leather luggage and headed back to palace life. After seeing how she'd faced down mold and maggots without flinching, he was forced to revise his timeframe.

Now, he'd give her a week.

He fished out some stick-on bandages and some antibiotic spray that had a numbing ingredient in it.

"This should help." Matt held out the first-aid supplies.

She reached out and took them with both hands. "Thank you. I appreciate you sharing your things with me."

Anneliese slid off the edge of the bed and winced as her boots hit the ground.

Matt eyed her skeptically. At the rate she was going, she wouldn't be able to make it back to her room to cover up the blisters. "Do you need me to help you?"

"Well, um…I don't think so." She tried to take another step toward the door. "Actually, it seems like I may be mistaken."

"Why don't you sit back there on the bed?" Matt pointed at the edge Anneliese had been sitting on, then pulled close the small chair from the table in the corner of the room. Gently, he lifted both of her legs into his lap and untied the laces of the heavy work boots.

He dropped each boot to the ground with a thud, then peeled off a pair of white cotton socks. Instantly, he felt sympathy for Anneliese. She had deep cuts on the back of each foot over the Achilles' tendon, bruises on the ball of each foot under the big toe, and the skin on the left pinky toe had been rubbed raw.

But the one thing he didn't see was fancy polish on her toenails. That surprised him. What kind of princess didn't get regular pedicures? Not that he knew any other princesses—but there had been plenty of girls in his social circle over the years who *thought* they were princesses, and they would never have dreamed of leaving the house without their toes touched up.

"You don't wear work boots often, do you?" He smiled as he reached for the spray, trying to reassure her. "This will probably sting a bit, but then it will numb out the area."

She bit her lower lip as the spray made contact with her injured skin. "No. This is actually a first for me. I guess you wear them a lot?"

He laughed as he peeled open the paper cover from the first bandage and wiggled his foot out to the side where she could see it. "Pretty much every day. I've had this pair for close to ten years."

He stretched a bandage over the cut at the back of one foot and pressed to get it to adhere. Her feet were very narrow and long. Delicate, even—except that was a strange way to think about a foot.

"I feel like I need a glass slipper right now."

Anneliese gave him a half smile, and he felt stupid for even saying that. Princess jokes. She'd probably heard them all before.

"They're not very forgiving or comfortable." Her reply was to-the-point.

He stretched the last bandage over another injured spot. "You're serious?"

She closed her eyes for a moment before answering, as though lost in thought. "Once. They were actually crystal." Then she shook her head. "It's not something that will ever be happening again."

The finality in her statement made Matt want to know the story behind it. But he didn't feel like a few adhesive bandages gave him the right to pry for more details.

"I think you're all set." He patted the top of her right foot.

She wiggled her toes. "Thank you. I'm sure this will be a big help."

Anneliese lifted her feet out of Matt's lap and lowered them to the floor. She gave the work boots and dirty socks a skeptical look.

"No one's going to know if you walk out of here barefoot, you know."

Her eyes opened wide, and a smile spread across her face. "I guess they wouldn't, would they?"

"Nope. No paparazzi here."

Her relief floated out on a sigh. "That's lovely. I hate paparazzi."

"Do you deal with it a lot?" Matt wondered what it would be like to live his life in a fishbowl. Here on Port Provident, he was a member of one of the island's oldest families, so he attracted some attention. But he didn't carry the Peoples family name, so for the most part, he'd always been able to slide under the radar.

"Moreso in the last year or two." She tucked a humidity-curled stray lock of hair behind her ear. "Heartbreak sells. Princess heartbreak sells the best."

Her voice fell almost to a whisper as she finished her sentence. Matt didn't know anything about her, but something inside felt sorry for her. He quickly brushed the thought away. Why would you ever feel sorry for a princess?

She stopped as she put her hand on the doorknob. "Do you know if there's a place to eat around here? I assume most of the restaurants are closed."

"They're pretty much all still closed, although I hear a few will be re-opening in the next week or so. This motel isn't much, but it's owned by the family that owns Porter's Seafood next door. They haven't opened to the public, but they have been putting out a small breakfast of mostly pre-packaged pastries and coffee in the mornings and a limited buffet at night for the people staying here. You're pretty much on your own for lunch, though. The grocery store hasn't re-opened yet. Most of us are getting meals here at Porter's and from the Samaritan's Cross truck as it goes through the neighborhood."

"The Samaritan's Cross truck?"

"It's a mobile kitchen that comes out to most disaster and emergency sites. Do you not have them in Saint Pedro?"

"It's San Petro," she gently corrected. "And no, I guess not. We haven't had a hurricane hit our island in a long time. We've had minor damage and glancing blows, but nothing like what Hurricane Hope brought here. Tell me, please, where is this dinner buffet?"

At the sound of the word 'dinner,' Matt heard his stomach rumble. "It's near the front office. I'm going to head that way. I can show you if you'd like."

"That would be lovely, thank you."

She followed him down the stairs and around the perimeter of the grounds until they came to the room that was set up every night for guests' meals. He never turned around to make sure she still followed, and strangely, he noticed that he never heard the sound of footsteps.

It kept making him think of Cinderella. He hadn't seen the movie since he was a kid. Forced to watch it with a sister who was full of thoughts on princesses and fairy godmothers and coaches made out of pumpkins, Matt had always been bothered by the rags-to-riches story. It just didn't fit his nature. Growing up, he'd played football. Now he built homes. Even though members of his family were considered wealthy in this town, Matt had always believed in working hard, getting dirty, and achieving your goals.

But, he wondered—what would it be like to have grown up like Anneliese de Cotriaro, to have everything you wanted and nothing denied?

Anneliese looked around the crowded room and felt a long way from home. As the thought settled on her heart, suddenly her whole mood changed.

She *was* a long way from home. She'd done it. She'd left San Petro on her own terms and had arrived in Port Provident to make the change she knew she was capable of making. There was more to Her Royal Highness Princess Anneliese Maria Evangelica Constantina de Cotriaro of San Petro than people were allowed to see.

She was more than a photograph taken with a long lens. She was more than a story quoting un-named palace sources. And she was definitely more than the former fiancée of Prince Rafael of Mardelago.

Anneliese made her way down the buffet line, carefully assessing each dish.

"What's that?"

Matt stopped and looked in the metal chafing dish. "Chicken fried chicken and gravy."

She studied the breaded cutlet a little more intently.

"So it's chicken, fried like chicken?" That made absolutely no sense.

"More or less." The corner of Matt's mouth inched up into a smile. He had a five o'clock shadow that was quickly moving to a six-or-seven o'clock shadow, and when the barest hint of white teeth showed in the middle, he looked like a pirate. "I think it's essentially a play on chicken fried steak, but just made with chicken instead. Fried chicken would be bone-in pieces of chicken, cut up and fried—like drumsticks or wings. This is a boneless, skinless chicken breast."

She followed him down the line. She recognized green beans and put a spoonful at the top of her plate. "What's a chicken fried steak?"

He stopped his progress down the buffet line and turned. "You've never had a chicken fried steak?"

"I'm afraid not."

"I feel a little sad for your country." He kept the smile on his face, so she knew he continued to joke. "It's a batter-dipped steak cutlet that is deep-fried. Top it with some gravy and make sure you have mashed potatoes on the side, and you have Texan perfection on a plate."

It sounded a bit like what they would call a *Milanesa de res* at home, but you definitely wouldn't put gravy on that.

"Tell me, do you have *chilaquiles en mole* for breakfast?" Her mouth watered at just the thought of her favorite morning meal, drizzled with the spicy chocolate-based sauce and crema, then topped with a dusting of paper-thin white onions and a splash of julienned cilantro.

"*Chile* what? Is that like some *chile con queso* thing?"

This time, it was Anneliese's turn to smile. "I feel a little sad for your country too."

"Touché." He pointed toward the back of the room. "There are two open chairs at that corner table. You're welcome to sit with me if you'd like."

Anneliese nodded and followed behind him, then hesitated for a second before realizing no one would be there to pull her chair out. She couldn't expect Matt to do it. No one was here to serve her.

She had come to serve others.

Cautiously, she tried the chicken fried chicken and quickly discovered the light batter and the juicy chicken tasted far better than she'd dreamed it could when she had put it on her plate.

"If this is close to Texan perfection, I should stay here longer so I can eat more."

Matt wiped the corner of his mouth with a flimsy paper napkin. "How long are you staying for?"

"A week or two. Your main office was able to put together an itinerary for me that would let me help with one of the houses and take part in some activities to raise awareness for your mission."

"So you really want to work on the Solares house?" Matt studied her face, like he was looking for an answer beyond whatever words she would say. It felt like a test.

"Very much." She cut another bite of the chicken. "Having this experience is something I need to do."

"What kind of experience?" Matt's eyes squinted slightly.

How could she explain it to him without seeming crazy? It wasn't just about the houses. She needed to rebuild herself—but she couldn't tell a virtual stranger that.

He wouldn't understand that eating dinner from a buffet while sitting barefoot at a table and wiggling her toes was something she'd never been able to do before in her life. She couldn't explain to him what eating with plastic cutlery from a paper plate symbolized to her.

If Rafael could see her now, he'd laugh at her and spin some other story to sell through his so-called "sources" to the tabloids.

Her heart had been beaten up this year. But for a moment, she decided to speak straight from it to Matt McGregor. She couldn't say why, exactly. She'd been brought up to measure her words, to keep from putting too much out there.

But she'd also been raised to use sterling flatware and eat off the finest bone china. She'd never even seen a chicken fried like a chicken before tonight, much less eaten one.

And it was wonderful.

Freedom lived in this room, and the men and women gathered here didn't even know it. They could choose what they wanted off the buffet. They could sit where they wanted, next to whom they wanted, and talk about what they wanted.

Anneliese decided she could do exactly the same. This week, there was no disapproving fiancé, no self-absorbed brother, no paparazzi vultures out to find the biggest headline.

She would find her heart. And she would speak from it.

"I'm here for the people of San Petro. I want to know what resources are available, should we ever find ourselves in a crisis like this. We're a small country. We don't have all the big resources like America does. But I believe we could have a plan and take care of our people. My brother doesn't plan ahead. He lives day-to-day. We've never seen a major hurricane take a direct hit in his lifetime, so in his mind, the possibility simply doesn't exist. And if it does…well… someone will come to fix it for him. Someone always does. But I've seen that waiting for other people to fix your problems just causes different problems."

The one lesson Rafael had taught her—don't expect someone else to be the difference you need in your life. She knew now that she had to be her own biggest advocate.

And someday, she'd need to be San Petro's biggest advocate. She didn't know for what, exactly—but she knew they'd never be able to count on her brother.

"The other reason I'm here is part of that. There's a vote in Parliament soon. I'm older than my brother, yet due to our laws, he will inherit our throne. Baby boys jump over baby girls in the line of succession. That's why we have a Crown Prince and not a Crown Princess. But there are those in our country who see my brother's ways are not the best for our country. They have introduced a bill to change our succession policy. It would be based on age, not gender. I believe that I could be a good ruler for San Petro one day if this bill passed. And if someone asks me why they should vote for this change, I want to be able to answer them honestly, with specific examples. I'd like to show the ways I'm better than my brother for San Petro's future, and why the current law is outdated. There's no reason a man is better for that job simply because he's a man. I hope the things I learn here can be something I can show my people. I want them to understand I'm learning and growing so I can do better for them."

Matt sat up a little straighter in his chair, and the look which had been on his face went blank.

"So there's a chance you could rule San Petro?"

She smiled. She'd lived with the hope inside for so long, but had never voiced it. "Perhaps. If that's what the people of San Petro want. It would take a full parliamentary vote."

"And you think working here with us would help you with that?"

She took a sip of iced tea out of the Styrofoam cup that an attendant had brought to the table.

"I think who we are is informed and influenced by our experiences —all of them. I believe that God doesn't necessarily call the equipped, He equips the called. I want to make sure I'm equipped to serve the people of San Petro if my call ever comes."

3

"*How* long have you been waiting there?" The sky had finally settled from the pink of dawn to the gold of early morning when Matt walked up to the front door to the Solares house and saw Anneliese sitting on the front porch.

"Oh, I don't know. A little while. I've just been enjoying the quiet. There's been a little breeze in the trees and some birds singing as they fly by. It's been peaceful."

Matt stepped past her and went to unlock the door to the house. "I'm glad you got that in because today's going to be anything but peaceful. Everything has been ripped out. It's time to start hanging the new drywall."

Anneliese followed him inside. He could see clear from one end of the house to the other. From the outside, the house looked virtually like nothing had happened—if you ignored the trash piled on the front lawn—but on the inside, the bungalow had been taken down to studs and concrete. It was time to rebuild a safe, rehabilitated home for the three generations who called this place home.

Last night's conversation had turned over in Matt's mind far into the small hours of the morning. He wouldn't have ever thought it, but the princess seemed to have a lot to prove with her involvement in this project.

As did he.

And today, he had to prove that the crew could hang an entire house full of drywall, then tape and float it and get it ready to be sanded and painted…and then the next stage and the next and the next.

He had a better understanding of Anneliese's motivations after their conversation last night. But he needed to make sure he stayed focused on his own goals. This was his hometown, and he *would* make a difference for the people who lived here. And that meant Matt couldn't afford to have a member of the crew here not pulling their weight. Last night, Anneliese had spoken of her desire to learn as much as she could so she could take the experiences back to San Petro.

Well, today, she'd certainly have an experience.

"You ever hung drywall before?" Matt laughed to himself as he said it. He didn't even have to wait for the answer to know what it would be.

"Well…I don't think so," Anneliese said, looking around the room.

Matt pointed to the stack of white gypsum board in the corner of the living room near the fireplace. "That's drywall."

"Oh, I see," she said softly, clearly indicating that she could physically see it, but she wasn't quite sure about anything else. "So what do we do with it?"

"Well, first, we'll split the crew into groups. Some will hang, and some will be floaters."

"Floaters?" Her gaze narrowed. She seemed to be taking detailed mental notes.

"The float crew will finish the joints between the sheets of drywall with tape and drywall compound. They'll also fill in the dents where the screwheads are. We want a nice, even finish to the wall. We'll sand it down before painting—that will come next."

"You said some people will hang it? How does that happen?"

"We'll get it on the studs with drywall screws." Matt picked up a handful from the supplies on the floor and showed her the long cylinders with the thread wrapped around it.

She pinched one out of his hand and rolled it around in her palm. "So what do you need me to do?"

She'd said she came here to be hands-on, to learn. So Matt was going to give her the same answer he'd give any member of his crew today.

"You're going to hang drywall."

"So their walls aren't going to be higher than five-and-a-half feet?" A smile filled her whole face. She punctuated it with a gentle laugh.

Matt was entirely caught off guard. He hadn't expected her to crack a joke. He hadn't expected her to have a self-deprecating sense of humor. And he definitely hadn't expected her smile to be best described as "radiant."

"How about you work with me? We'll make sure their house isn't fit for Hobbits."

Something about Anneliese made Matt stop in his tracks. He'd noticed individual features on her before—like her tailored clothes and her blonde-streaked trendy haircut. But when she called attention to her whole figure and topped it off with a smile that shone like a diamond, he found himself looking at her differently. Completely.

Matt made himself go walk around the house, checking the stacks of drywall that had been delivered. He needed a change of scenery before he had the image of Anneliese stuck in his head for the rest of the day.

He told himself he didn't want to lose focus and injure himself with a drywall screw or other equipment today.

But that wasn't entirely it.

That wasn't it at all.

And the bigger problem was—he knew it.

Matt found himself very impressed with the speed and efficiency shown so far today by the full crew of Helping Hands team members and volunteers. He also found himself very impressed by his ability to not be distracted by Anneliese, even though she'd followed him like a shadow all day.

She was a consistent worker if a little timid. Matt had tried not to be on her case about little things, but he did decide early on that he'd provide her the same level of feedback that he'd provide any other crew member. He needed to be consistent both for his own peace of mind and to honor her desire to learn.

"Last couple of sheets and then we'll be through with this room. This came together faster than I'd thought it would."

Anneliese adjusted her grip and Matt heard a quiet "Oh shoot."

"What happened?'

"Nothing," she said with a small grunt. "Let's get this done."

Quickly, the sheet of gypsum board was affixed to the last open spot in the wall. As soon as her hands were free, Anneliese looked at her pointer finger.

Without warning, she stuck it in her mouth and chewed on the nail. Just as earlier—but for a whole different reason, now—Matt couldn't take his eyes off her.

She spat the nail fragment on the ground.

"What? It broke." The tone of her voice clearly signaled that she felt the simple statement explained it all.

"You're just the first princess I've ever seen chew her nails. Or spit."

Her Royal Highness raised her eyebrows and made a small, self-satisfied sound. "I'm the first princess you've ever seen. And I might just surprise you, Matt."

The gauntlet had been thrown.

And something told Matt that there was a good chance he'd enjoy the ride.

Anneliese found Matt in the backyard, talking to his team of Helping Hands Homes staff. She waited patiently in the shadow of a palm tree that had been stripped of most of its fronds by the recent violent winds.

"Matt?" she asked before he could get away.

"Hey, Anneliese. What'cha need?" He dropped his gaze to her hand. "Nail okay?"

She laughed a little. "Yes, it's fine. I don't anticipate needing an amputation."

"That's good. I have a safety record to maintain."

Anneliese gave him a knowing nod. "I definitely wouldn't want to do anything to jeopardize that. In fact, I thought that since you said we're a little ahead of schedule, well…I might check one of the boxes off my list.

She held out the itinerary she'd been given by the Helping Hands Homes main office when she first came to town.

"What do you mean?" Matt reached out and tipped the bottom edge of the paper up so that he could get a better look.

"This one right here." She tapped a line near the top of the page. "I don't have a specific appointment to visit this one, but it was highly recommended that I stop by and see this new thing called The Grace Space at a church not far from here."

Matt leaned a little closer. "Oh, *La Iglesia de la Luz del Mundo.* Yeah, that's just a handful of blocks from here. A lot of the people in this neighborhood attend church there. It's a centerpiece of the community."

"Supposedly they've integrated front-line medical care with a donated goods storefront. If it's okay with you, I thought I might go over and see what they're doing."

Matt's second-in-command, a man in his early twenties named Jacob, walked by. Matt caught him by his sleeve and leaned over and said something to him in low tones.

As Jacob walked off, Matt tapped the paper. "I'll drive you over there. It's not too far, but walking to *La Iglesia* would eat up time that you could spend actually learning about what they're doing."

"Are you sure?" He'd been so clear this morning about what all had to get completed at the Solares house today.

Matt reached in his pocket and pulled out his keys, tossing them in the air, then catching them. "Yes. I need to wait for all the plaster to dry that the float crew applied. Jacob is organizing groups to start laying down tile in the kitchen and the bathrooms, but those are both pretty tight spaces. So I think it's okay if we're down two people for an hour or so. Jacob's perfectly capable of sailing this ship."

"Well, if you're sure—let me go pick up my bag. I can meet you at your truck?"

"Sounds great. See you out front." He smiled.

Seeing the relaxed look on his face made Anneliese breathe a sigh of relief. She'd been unusually nervous about asking Matt if she could go see The Grace Space. She didn't want to be seen as not pulling her weight at the house.

In her world, people deferred to her—well, except for those like her brother and former fiancé. But if she wanted to go somewhere, do something, she didn't ask for permission. She asked someone to make it happen.

In Port Provident, though, she wasn't here as a princess. She was here as a servant of her people, here to learn, here to absorb. And in order to do what she'd come to do, she knew she needed Matt McGregor's support and partnership. They'd gotten off to a rocky start, but as the day had gone on today, Anneliese felt a change. Whatever had caused it, she wanted to make sure that the goodwill between them continued to grow. She'd get so much more out of her time here if it did.

Matt stood next to the open passenger-side door. "Hop on in."

"I'm not sure I'm much of a hopper."

"If you tried it, you might like it." He elbowed her as she came close to the front seat.

She couldn't help herself. She threw her head back and laughed. It felt good to let her control slip for just a moment. "I've never been much of a risk-taker."

Bracing his arm against the door jamb, Matt stared at her thoughtfully. "Why's that?"

Anneliese shrugged. How did she make him understand the conventions which had been drilled in her since birth? How did she make him understand the heartbreak of her last year without giving explanations she had no intention of giving?

"You just never really know who you're speaking to or who you're with."

His gaze didn't waver. "So you don't trust anyone, Anneliese?"

She paused before answering and ran through a list in her mind. When it came down to it, no one made the cut. There were a handful that she believed the best of, but in the end, she'd been let down enough that she knew everyone had a price—family, friends, strangers. No one was immune from it.

"Not really." She chose not to hop in the truck, but instead to climb in the same way she'd always been taught to—knees together, first foot on running board, second foot on running board, first foot on the floor mat, second foot on the floor mat, shift, sit, arrange feet.

Maybe someday she could just hop, she thought wistfully. But if she achieved her ultimate goal and Parliament voted her up in the succession, she knew that day would never come.

And duty to her country over self-desire always came first.

Even when it came to "hopping" into a vehicle.

Matt climbed in his side of the truck and started the engine without saying a word. They turned two corners before he spoke.

"So you wouldn't trust me?"

It didn't take more than a split second for her to answer. "I don't even know you. That's a silly question."

"I guess I just don't understand. I'm not the kind of guy who is filming reality TV-style confessionals, but I do have people I can talk to if I need them. It blows my mind that someone who could have anything in the world they wanted doesn't feel like there's anyone they can speak freely around."

"What makes you think I could have anything in the world I want?" The words tasted metallic as she spat them out. "See? Why would I trust you? You're just like everyone else. You've made up your mind about me, and you don't even know me."

Anneliese forced herself to bite her tongue. This was precisely the kind of situation she tried never to put herself in. Keep conversations polite and cordial. Speak formally. Never give in to emotions, never go below the surface. Let people hear what they want to hear so when your time together is through, there's nothing they could misunderstand or twist and give to a hungry reporter as a juicy soundbite.

"How could anyone get to know you if you're always holding something back?" Matt pulled into the parking lot beside the church.

His question was thrown like an inside pitch in baseball. It made her jump back and think about where she stood. She didn't like the pressure she felt when she tried to explain it to herself. None of her answers sounded right. And if they didn't make sense to her, they weren't going to make sense when they came out of her mouth.

Maybe the best decision was to just go with the tried-and-true method—just keep her mouth shut.

"So you're not going to answer me?" He shifted the car into park after pulling into a space on the front row.

"Why should I? I don't know you."

"If that's your circular logic, then you'll spend your whole life in your bubble. And one day, you'll look around you and wonder why life passed you by, princess life or no princess life."

He spoke with a conviction Anneliese wished her own words contained.

She put her hand on the door, wanting to get out of the truck, but hesitating. "How do you know?"

Matt had turned off the engine. The truck was silent except for the squawk of a seagull in the distance and the sound of Matt's own voice. "Have you ever heard of C.S. Lewis?"

Anneliese lowered her hand from the door handle. She couldn't figure out where Matt was going with this shift in the direction of the conversation. "*Narnia, The Screwtape Letters*—of course."

"My great-aunt loves his works. She's probably read them all. I used to spend a lot of time with her when I was younger, and she was always handing off books for me to read. She handed off a lot of C.S. Lewis. One of his ideas has stuck with me since I first read it as a teenager."

"What is that?"

"Well, I'll probably get it wrong if I try to quote it. You can read it yourself in his book *The Four Loves* if you want to get the quote right. But the gist of it is this—a friendship starts when someone says something and the other person realizes they're not alone, they have something in common that they didn't think they shared with anyone else."

She had to admit it—that was an interesting thought. "I can see what he's saying there."

"But Anneliese, you've got to live it. If you don't ever put yourself out there, you won't have those lightbulb moments, those flashes where you realize 'this person gets me'."

"Matt, I understand what you're saying. But your world and my world are very different."

He nodded. "You're probably right. But you're in my world for now. You ought to give it a try."

Inside the building, Matt went in search of Pastor Marco Ruiz so he could make introductions to Anneliese.

The familiar sound of Spanish filled pockets of the air. It sounded like home.

"*Hola, Querida.*" An older woman with her hair pulled up in a bun walked over to Anneliese. Her face was lit with a smile that matched the sweet Spanish endearment she offered as a greeting. "I'm Inez Vasquez. Welcome to The Grace Space. How can I help you? Are you looking for something for your home, or are you here to see one of the doctors in the medical clinic? Also, the members of our church are cooking a hot meal outside. Don't forget to stop by on your way out. It will be a simple meal, but we promise it will fill your belly."

Anneliese felt completely comfortable here. It was like doing a visit to a charity back in San Petro, and she'd been doing those since she was old enough to assume full royal duties. She answered back in Spanish, thanking the woman for her hospitality.

"My friend is looking for Pastor Ruiz." Anneliese hesitated a minute as she realized she'd called Matt her friend. She shrugged it off, not knowing what else she could have said that wouldn't have sounded awkward.

"I think he's in the clinic with Dr. Shipley. While you're waiting, please take a look around." Mrs. Vasquez gestured around what had likely once been the main sanctuary of the church, but was now set up to look more like a store, with chairs and pews and tables assembled to form rows for merchandise instead of places for people to sit.

"Thank you, I will. It looks like you all have put in a lot of hard work here."

"Oh yes, we have. Dr. Shipley pulled together a great idea to fill in several gaps in the community." She paused and studied Anneliese's face. "Has anyone ever told you that you look like Princess Anneliese of San Petro?"

Anneliese froze. She knew she'd been at that press conference, and eventually, people would figure out she was here, but she wasn't ready to give up the semi-anonymity she assumed she'd have since most people on the island still didn't have access to televisions and other news sources with regularity yet.

"I've heard that, *sí.*"

Mrs. Vasquez sighed. "I love her. She's beautiful and so classy. I think it's awful how Prince Rafael treated her. Who would do something like that to someone as lovely as her?"

The words from this complete stranger washed over her like a spring rain.

"It's hard to believe, isn't it?" They were the first words she'd uttered in her own defense in this whole crazy year, and they felt good to say.

They felt amazingly good to say.

In fact, Anneliese felt a glow inside. There were people out there who saw Rafael's actions for what they were. In a small way, she felt that light switch Matt had talked about earlier flip on.

.   .   .

"Anneliese, I'd like you to meet Pastor Marco Ruiz and Dr. Pete Shipley." Matt walked up with two men following closely behind. "Pastor Ruiz, Dr. Shipley, this is…"

Anneliese jumped in when Matt hesitated. She put out her hand to Pastor Ruiz first. "Anneliese de Cotriaro."

Out of the corner of her eye, Anneliese saw the older woman's jaw drop. "*Qué?*"

Anneliese gave her a sideways smile.

"It's nice to meet you, Miss de Cotriaro," the pastor said, taking her hand between both his own and giving a peaceful shake.

She shook the doctor's hand next and exchanged pleasantries with him. "Let me give you a tour of what we're doing here, Miss de Cotriaro," he said with evident pride in the operation around him.

As they began to walk toward a sign at the back labeled "Clinic," Anneliese noticed Mrs. Vasquez had stepped away from their small group and was walking as fast as she could back toward the front counter where some other ladies were working.

So much for that dose of anonymity. *Abuelas* at a church supper could spread any word faster than any satellite feed from a news station could ever hope to.

Dr. Shipley gave a brief overview of how The Grace Space came to be. "I came to volunteer one day to help sort a truck's worth of items that had been donated here to La Iglesia. As I worked, more donations kept coming in. It didn't take long to see we were quickly going to be overwhelmed with the volume of generosity. Then, as I got to know some of the church members who were gathering here, it also became clear we were on the verge of a health crisis with the hospital closed indefinitely. A community gathering place that allowed people to take what they need and get access to basic medical checks and medications would fill a huge hole in the community."

"And has it worked as you had hoped, Dr. Shipley?"

"Please just call me Pete—we're not standing on formality here—only grace, as the name implies. But to answer your question, yes. We have steady traffic in here all day long. I can see this becoming a more long-term thing, but right now, I don't see how that happens. So we'll continue doing the best we can with what we have right now."

Matt jumped into the conversation. "And everything is run by volunteers?"

Pete nodded. "One hundred percent. Volunteers from the church sort and stock our makeshift store aisles. Doctors and medical residents who are not in their full-time roles due to the shutdown at the hospital and medical school are staffing the clinic. And the ladies' group from *La Iglesia* prepares meals daily. And we've got support from churches across the state of Texas to bring us donated goods to stock and food to cook, as well as partnerships with some mobile clinics and pharmacies from Houston that have graciously donated their medical equipment. It's amazing how it's all come together in such a short period of time."

Anneliese looked around the open area. She could see the citizens of San Petro coming together to create a place like this if there was a need. Federico would sit back and wait for aid from foreign governments and large groups. But why? Clearly, some strategic thinking and willing hands were all one would need.

"This is very impressive, Dr. Shipley...I mean, Pete. And you have much to be proud of with the members of your church, Pastor Ruiz." Anneliese smiled as she made her mental notes.

From a morning of drywall to making time for this tour, it had been a long day, and it was only mid-afternoon. But the adhesive bandages on her feet were holding up nicely, and there was optimism in her heart.

"Before you go, please stop and grab a bite to eat from the ladies of *La Iglesia*. The ministry we perform out there is just as important as what we're doing in here," Pastor Ruiz said. "We're providing a place where people can meet two very basic needs—food and community. I feel like we're getting to the heart of many of the same things Jesus did as he met people and performed his ministry. We're not exactly transforming loaves and fishes, but we are transforming lives at a time when people really need hope."

As Anneliese and Matt walked through the line, each picking up a simple plate of tortillas and rice and beans, the pastor's words stuck with her.

"Excuse me for a moment, Matt." Instead of heading for one of the small tables, Anneliese walked to the corner of the lawn in search of Pastor Ruiz. He stood talking to a lady with long dark hair. She was dressed casually in jeans and a T-shirt, but the look on her face was serious.

"Oh, Anneliese," Pastor Ruiz waved her into the conversation. "This is my aunt, City Councilwoman Angela Ruiz.

"His much younger aunt," she said with the hint of a laugh. "It's the family joke, but it's true."

"It's very nice to meet you," Anneliese said. She realized she was still holding the plate of food and a can of soda, so she couldn't properly shake hands. It felt a little strange to not exchange a formal greeting, but then again, today she was just trying to be Anneliese—not all the other baggage that usually came along with her on an official charity visit.

"Can I answer a question for you, Anneliese?" Pastor Ruiz said kindly.

"You mentioned the story of the loaves and fishes earlier and how you felt the same about the work you were doing here. I was hoping you could elaborate some on that role in the community. Where I come from, the church is very much a part of our history, but I don't know if it's truly an inspirational force anymore. Would you say things are different here?"

"In our particular community, absolutely. The neighborhoods that surround *La Iglesia* are multi-generational. There's a lot of personal investment here. And our church has been a constant presence for decades. We're not just a place where people go on Sundays. We're ladies' Bible studies during the week and summer picnics at the beach and meals when someone is sick or has a new baby." He gestured at the small but social crowd on the lawn.

"I'm fond of quoting Proverbs 27:17—'As iron sharpens iron, so one man sharpens another.' Of course, that extends to women and children, too." He smiled. "We're about not just teaching the truth of

Jesus here, but creating the relationships that help people live their best lives."

Her earlier conversation with Matt filtered through Anneliese's mind. "Friendship," she said simply.

"Absolutely," Pastor Ruiz answered. "And what better friend do we have than Jesus? If we set the right example, the rest of it falls into place."

Anneliese filed the pastor's words away in her heart. It made so much sense. Her beloved island was following the examples of those in leadership now. Her old and frail father who rarely left the palace anymore—he wasn't an example, his people no longer saw him. And then there was the heir-apparent, Federico, who wasn't an example to the people of San Petro either. Well, he did set an example—but it mostly read like a laundry list of things not to emulate.

She had been turned off by her brother's example for years. And now she knew why.

The city councilwoman addressed Anneliese. "You're Princess Anneliese of San Petro, correct? I recognize you from photos."

There was no use in denying it. It wasn't entirely unexpected that a congregation of people who spoke Spanish and had ties to Mexico and Latin America would know who she was. Slipping under the radar had been nice while it lasted, but there wasn't a way she could deny who she was without lying, and she could never do that.

"I am," she answered simply. "Although I'm here for personal, not official reasons, so my trip has not been publicized outside of a brief press conference I participated in on behalf of Helping Hands Homes after my arrival."

Angela nodded in understanding. "I respect that. I know your capital city of Rosada is one of our sister cities, so I do thank you for coming—whatever your reasons are. We will have some more special guests on the island tomorrow, so you're not the only one trying to come in under the radar and see how they can help Port Provident recover."

Anneliese thanked Pastor Ruiz again for his time and hospitality and gave her best wishes to Angela for the work she knew the city government would be facing in the weeks and months ahead. As she walked back to where Matt was sitting, talking to a group of church members.

"I'll get our main office to send someone over here and help the *La Iglesia* community sign up for home renovations. We have a big goal to touch a lot of lives here, and I know the Alamo Court neighborhood has been hit hard, so of course, we want as many of you to apply as possible. I'll get someone out here with hard copy forms and the knowledge to walk you through the process."

Anneliese quietly took the open seat next to Matt and let him finish his conversation with the ladies. They all looked at her with dropped jaws, but then scrambled away to their volunteer stations without addressing her directly.

"I'm glad you wanted to come out here, Anneliese. Seeing the work they've done here to put together The Grace Space is inspiring. And it's given me a chance to spread the word about the work we're doing with Helping Hands Homes, too. The more good people we get to help, the better."

"Iron sharpening iron?" Everything seemed to be tying together today.

Matt took a bite of flour tortilla and chewed carefully before answering. "I think so. There are so many good-hearted people in this community. If you give them the opportunities to support and serve, to be a part of something beyond themselves, they'll do it. And then that gives you more opportunities to help more people and bring more new skills and views on board to push the cycle even further."

"I like that explanation. I've made so many mental notes today. I wish I'd brought an actual notebook."

"I think I have one at the hotel. It's yours if you need it." Matt twisted open a bottle of water.

"I met a member of city council while I was talking to Pastor Ruiz. She said some other special visitors are coming to town tomorrow. She didn't say who they were, but it seems like more good things may be happening."

As she said that, Anneliese realized she couldn't stop herself from looking at Matt. He didn't have to treat her like one of the crew, but he had. He hadn't placed her behind a glass case. He'd laid out his expectations and let her spread her wings.

She studied his features—the flint-gray eyes, the sharp angles of his chin. She saw something strong and honorable in Matt McGregor. Could it be that he was the very iron she needed in her path to make this time in Port Provident as sharp an influence as it could be in her life?

4

———————

"Change of plans." Dave found Matt in the bathroom shower, finishing up a line of tile grout.

"We had plans?" His boss seemed clearly flustered, and the only thing Matt could think of was how funny he found it.

Dave shot him a no-nonsense look. "They're coming here in less than an hour. We just got the call from the Port Provident Public Information Officer. I got in my car and came over here as fast as I could."

Matt laid his supplies carefully at his feet in the pan of the shower. "I still have no idea what you're talking about."

"The presidents." Dave threw the noun out there like that explained it all. "FPOTUSes"

"Watch your mouth, Dave. Don't you FPOTUS me." Matt decided he was just going to yank Dave's chain early and often if these were the kinds of responses he was going to get. "You're gonna have to come again."

Dave spoke slowly, as if the comprehension problem between the two of them happened to do with the speed of his speech. "Former presidents Bill Foster and Mark George. Pretty sure you've heard of them. They're doing an aerial tour of the island right now with the

44

Foster/George Gulf Coast Recovery Fund. After they land, there's a photo op with them on the beach, then they're coming here. To the Solares house. They want to see what Helping Hands is doing."

And just like that, the whole game changed.

The two former presidents had teamed up to raise money for the Gulf Coast after hurricanes in recent years, and they had historically been keenly focused on housing restoration. In the two most recent hurricanes, Matt's projects had received grants from the fund that had gone a long way to achieving goals.

With the Port Provident rebuild commitment being the most ambitious ever targeted by Helping Hands Homes, Matt knew a good impression could make or break their fundraising goals.

"Now I understand." Matt looked down at his grout-swiped T-shirt and wished he had a change of clothes. "We need a game plan, don't we?"

"Exactly." Dave said. "I knew you'd come around."

Anneliese planed the scraper along the last of the porch rail, peeling back the old paint and sending shavings to tumble by her feet like snow. She'd spent most of the day out on the front porch scraping and sanding. It was reasonably mundane work, but it gave her time to think more about what she'd seen and heard yesterday.

The key, she felt strongly, was to be found in creating community —a situation where the strengths of everyone could be maximized and mobilized for the good of themselves and their neighbors. Matt had talked about the "*a ha!*" moment of friendship, but clearly, there were so many other opportunities to create moments like that.

She'd just need to find the right ones when she returned to San Petro. They wouldn't need to wait for a moment of crisis—if they laid the groundwork now, they could reap the benefits sooner and stand taller if a crisis did come—as well as provide tangible benefits in the meantime.

The rumble of engines disrupted the quiet of the neighborhood and

Anneliese's thoughts. As she looked toward the end of the street, four large, black SUVs with deeply tinted windows came to a stop directly across the street from the Solares house.

Men in dark suits and crisp white shirts stepped out first. Obviously, they weren't from around here. There weren't many working washers and dryers in Port Provident right now, much less cans of starch to make shirt collars stand at attention.

Anneliese watched intently. She'd spent her life riding in vehicles like this, with these same type of men getting out ahead of her.

A watery feeling rumbled in the pit of her stomach. Had these men been sent to bring her home? She had left word that all communications with her needed to funnel through her secretary, Carlos. Could her brother Federico have become so angered by that directive that he sent people to bring her back to San Petro?

Or worse—would he have shown up here himself?

The faces that stepped out of the center SUV were both familiar to Anneliese, but neither had come on a flight from San Petro. She recognized former United States presidents Bill Foster and Mark George. Both had come on official visits to San Petro during their respective presidencies. Former President Foster had also brought his family to vacation on her Caribbean island, and she and her family had all been guests of President Foster when he'd been in the White House.

When she saw City Councilwoman Angela Ruiz step out of another one of the SUVs, along with a few others, Anneliese realized the two former presidents must have been the special guests Angela Ruiz alluded to during yesterday's conversation at *La Iglesia de la Luz del Mundo*.

She was covered in paint flecks and probably had a gallon's worth of sweat soaking her clothes, but Anneliese remembered how important the special visit had seemed to Angela Ruiz. If she could help in any way, she would. She was here to lend her support to whatever Port Provident needed.

Anneliese walked off the porch, down the sidewalk, and headed directly toward two of the most powerful men on earth with her head held high.

"Your Highness, Princess Anneliese?" A look of recognition that battled with disbelief came over the face of Former President Mark Foster.

"President Foster, it's so nice to see you again." She put out her hand, and President Foster picked it up and gave a delicate kiss of greeting on the back of her knuckles. "And President George, it's an equal pleasure to see you as well."

The other man repeated the same affectionate greeting. Anneliese laughed at herself. Scraping paint and hanging drywall were skills she had to learn. But to talk with two men who had each worn the mantel of "Leader of the Free World"?

That was practically an innate skill.

"As you may know, San Petro's capital city of Rosada is a sister city to Port Provident, so I wanted to I'm working this week with Helping Hands Homes. They've set a goal to rehabilitate 100 homes in Port Provident by Christmas. This particular home belongs to the Solares family. With the Helping Hands Homes crew and a team of dedicated volunteers, we are on track to have them home in a matter of days. Would you like a tour?"

"Absolutely." President Foster started toward the house, and President George followed a hair behind Anneliese. The rest of the city dignitaries and others all fell into line behind the *de facto* tour guide.

When they walked inside, Matt and David were huddled in a corner, talking animatedly.

"President Foster, President George, I'd like to introduce you to David Long, CEO of Helping Hands Homes, and Matt McGregor, president of the division covering the southern United States." Anneliese waited for David and Matt to notice the group. "David, Matt, I'd like to introduce both of you to former U.S. Presidents Bill Foster and Mark George. They're touring the island today and stopped by."

As soon as the pleasantries were completed, Matt took over the tour. He pointed out specifics of the remodel and began to break down just what would be necessary to replicate this goal ninety-nine more times across Port Provident.

"This is my hometown, and so it's a privilege for me to be able to provide a helping hand to the residents of Port Provident. But because we do these repairs at low-or-no-cost to the homeowners, it's important that we build awareness as far and wide as we can." Matt leaned against the mantel that had just been re-installed over the fireplace. "Gentlemen, I'm very glad to have you here today. It's been a privilege to show you around the Solares house and talk about our operation. But I'd also like to ask for your support to spread the word about what we're doing here. Additionally, we've already put in a funding request through your Gulf Coast Recovery Fund, and I'd like to respectfully request your consideration. We could shift our plan to a much higher gear with more awareness and more funds."

President George nodded his head. "Absolutely. This is the kind of project we are looking to support. It's hands-on, uses volunteers from the community, and can make an impact before the government can even find the scissors to try and cut the red tape."

"Exactly. And it's easy to see why people like Princess Anneliese back a project like this." President Foster picked up where his counterpart left off, then looked over his shoulder. "Ellen, when you get back to the office, can you find the paperwork Mr. McGregor was referencing? Let's expedite the process and get Helping Hands as much funding as we can get to them under our rules and charter."

Anneliese watched as Matt's face transformed through a business-like seriousness as he gave the tour, to listening with intent as the former Presidents gave their thoughts, to a wave of relief as the Helping Hands Homes funding request was green-lighted by one of the men with his name on the foundation.

Some of that wave of happiness washed over to her as well. She hoped that in some small way, she'd been able to play a part in what just happened—that her presence here had been for a reason and had been useful.

She hoped she'd been iron today.

Matt scanned the hotel dining area, looking for Anneliese. He didn't see her anywhere. On his way to a table, he caught a glance out the main window. He saw a solitary figure pause on the sidewalk, look both ways to survey the traffic on Gulfview Boulevard, and then cross the street with bare feet.

He turned back to the line and went in search of a Styrofoam to-go container for his dinner.

"Is this seat taken?" Matt padded up next to where Anneliese had perched herself on a granite boulder.

She looked up at him and smiled. "Not for the right company."

Matt turned his head left, then right. "Well, I don't see Prince Charming coming, so I guess you're stuck with me."

"Prince Charming is a myth. There are no white horses. Just bratty boys living in men's bodies driving fast cars and going from one self-centered activity to the next." Her shoulders slumped heavily as she spit out the indictment.

"I would have thought someone like you wouldn't have trouble finding an eligible bachelor."

"Someone like me? I'm not entirely sure what you think about my life, Matt, but it's not my own." She put down the burger she'd been eating. "My secretary plans my daily schedule. My dresser picks my clothes. My parents selected where I went to school and dropped strong hints about what I should study. They decided on my relationship with Rafael. My mother died of cancer—even being a queen couldn't save her. And my father had a stroke the same day I ended my engagement."

"So how'd you get to come here?" Matt asked. He hadn't expected the force in her answer.

"I didn't tell anyone. I had my private secretary set it up, but I swore him to secrecy. He's new to working with me, but he's loyal. He wouldn't sell me out to the tabloids—or my brother, who's taken over most of my father's duties since the stroke. And then I turned off my cell phone."

"So you're a runaway princess?"

"I prefer the term 'runaway humanitarian.' I really did come here to help." She looked out toward the horizon and the constant roll of the waves. "You know, this is my first time in Texas, but I've always been fascinated by it here."

Matt picked up his burger but paused before taking a bite. "How so?"

"Well, I haven't seen anyone riding a horse yet, so that's been a little disappointing. But I remember reading a book when I was much younger about the Alamo and Texas history. I was fascinated by the larger-than-life descriptions, the bravery, the heroism. The fact that people say everything is bigger in Texas—I've always wanted to see for myself if it's true."

"And is it?" Matt had grown up with a fascination with the history of the Lone Star State himself, but he'd always attributed it to living here his whole life and being a descendant of people who had helped shape Texas history after the Great Storm of 1915 here in Port Provident.

"I haven't seen enough of Texas to really judge, but I think it just might be so. I've seen that Texans have big hearts. Everyone has been so friendly—and I haven't really heard the word 'no,' even with all the work to be done and all the needs that are around every corner on this island. There's a can-do spirit, a belief that what needs to be done will get done. I'd like to be princess of a place like this."

"A Texas princess?"

"Absolutely. And I'd build a palace right here where I could watch the sun rise and set every day over the water. The water speaks to my soul. Granted, San Petro definitely has the edge on watercolor compared to what you have here in Port Provident."

Matt laughed. "You're a princess. Fix it."

"That's on God's checklist, not mine. But everything I've read says there's no place like Texas, so it looks like he did an A-plus job on everything else, nature-wise here. We'll let the fact that the water isn't Caribbean blue slide a little bit."

Matt finished his burger and fries and enjoyed the quiet moment of watching Anneliese watch the waves. She said the water spoke to her soul. The longer he was around Anneliese de Cotriaro—just Anneliese, not Her Royal Highness Princess Anneliese—he realized *she* spoke to his soul.

She was guarded. She measured her words carefully and spoke more formally than most people in his circle. She didn't know the first thing about construction work.

But it didn't matter.

She gave her all to everything she did, whether that was thinking about the words she said, traveling far from home to see conditions in a sister city first hand, or spitting a manicured fingernail on the concrete floor after it had gotten hung up and broken on the edge of a sheet of drywall.

Truly, Matt didn't think he knew anyone like Anneliese.

"I actually came over here to thank you," he said after a seagull's squawk broke through the silence.

"To thank me?"

The city-wide dawn-to-dusk curfew had been lifted earlier today, and Matt was enjoying being back out in the moonlight, watching the play of the orb's glow on Anneliese's dark blonde hair. Her naturally tanned skin was kissed by pale highlights in the hollows and curves.

"Yeah, Dave's already gotten a call from the presidential foundation office. They're expediting the paperwork—as former President George asked—but they're also sending a check by the end of next week so we can keep moving forward. I don't think that would have happened without your prior relationship with both of them and the poise and hospitality you showed today."

She smoothed her hair back as the breeze tried to make it dance. "I really didn't do anything."

"You did, and I know it."

Matt wanted her to take the credit she deserved. He wanted her to understand he wasn't just saying something he didn't mean.

He leaned over and wrapped an arm around her shoulders and pulled her slightly to the right for a hug. He felt her curves melt up against his ribcage and he squeezed just a little with the fingers that were wrapped around the gentle roll of the cap of her shoulder.

He felt as peaceful and perfect as the waves that rose and fell in front of them.

At the pressure of his fingertips, Anneliese stiffened and twisted so she put space in between them.

"I'm sorry." Conflict split down the center of Matt's mind. He wasn't sorry for himself, for the quiet perfection of spirit that had settled in him as he took Anneliese in his arms. But he was sorry if she hadn't felt that same pull of quiet electricity. "There are probably rules about that sort of things. Probably way too friendly for a princess and a guy who builds things with his hands."

Anneliese lifted his hand from her shoulder. Surprisingly, she didn't drop it, though. She held it in her own hand and stared. Her thumb traced a new scab down the side of Matt's own thumb.

"That's not it at all."

"It's not?" The effect of the gentle smoothing of the pad of her thumb against the rough line of the scab meant he had to force his concentration.

She stopped the movement of her thumb but didn't release his hand from her own. "No. You were just being a friend."

Matt wasn't so sure about that anymore, but he held back the thoughts rising in his head.

"I don't have a lot of close friends," she admitted. "And after my engagement ended, I lost a number of the ones I had thought I could call mine. Rafael said some ugly things about me, had his surrogates sell out 'exclusives' to the tabloids and gossip magazines. I refused to throw any mud. I kept my silence. I didn't see the point in defending myself against lies. But very few people spoke up for me—publicly or privately. I think I have to learn to trust people again. At least I hope that I can."

He took his hand back, and placed one hand on each of her shoulders, then turned Anneliese so that she faced him. He wanted to see her moonlit face—and he wanted to make sure that she saw his, that she heard his words.

"The only magazine I read is *This Old House*. I don't know who your ex-fiancé is and I don't know what people said about you. But I do know what it means to be a true friend. And if you need a friend, it would be an honor to be one for you."

Anneliese reached up and gently put her arms around Matt's neck, then leaned in with a soft pull toward her.

"Thank you," she said. The whisper of her words brushed against his neck.

Matt lowered his head to hers, and his cheek brushed against the silk of her blonde hair. He could smell a faint whiff of perfume—the powder and floral mixing with a stronger scent of a long day's work. It seemed to sum up all the contradictions about this princess who'd come to Texas.

Well, it summed up all the mysteries except for one—what was he going to do when she went back home?

5

―――――

"*M*att, no, I'm sorry, I just can't." Anneliese poured coffee into a travel cup and pressed a lid down tightly.

"Anneliese, I think this would be another great opportunity for the charity. It would be great for people to hear straight from you why you're lending your support to Helping Hands Homes."

She felt her short ponytail swish with defiance as she shook her head. "I said no. I am not here to do interviews."

Matt sat his to-go cup of coffee on the table, right next to hers. "You appeared at the press conference the first day you were here."

"That was different. I didn't really have a choice, and I didn't have much of a speaking role. They needed me, and I agreed to it. But I didn't come here to be on a media tour. I'm not the biggest fan of the media—I explained that to you."

"Will you at least come with me to the event this morning? I left Jacob in charge again so we could go. He'll have the crew installing cabinets and painting walls today."

She considered throwing the bagel in her hand at him—she was not a fan of being pestered like this. But then thoughts of last night—of the water, the moon, and the feel of security as they lingered for a moment in each other's embrace—came back to her. Matt had said he wanted to be her friend.

And she'd made her heart quietly admit that she wanted to claim his friendship too.

Anneliese knew this trip would come to an end and she'd be returning to San Petro, so she knew she couldn't let the thoughts in her mind wander past the simple agreement of friendship they'd talked through last night.

She owed it to Matt to support the things that were important to him because that's what a friend would do—just so long as she didn't have to speak publicly to anyone.

The oversized sliding doors between the three main ballrooms at the Grand Provident hotel had all been opened, creating one large room. Rows and rows and rows of tables snaked across the room—up and down and back again.

The Port Provident Recovery Fair was designed to bring agencies and resources together under one roof so that the residents of Port Provident could easily find the help they would need to navigate insurance, red tape, and recovery.

Matt pulled out the first chair at the table which had been placed in the Helping Hands Homes booth. Their setup wasn't fancy—white and green pipe and drape with two tall full-color banners brought in from the Houston regional office—but it was clean, and the table held a number of brochures and flyers which would easily answer questions residents might have about the program.

"Thank you," Anneliese murmured as she sat down and let Matt scoot the chair close to the table. She didn't know how much information she could impart to passers-by, but Matt had been right earlier. Being here today would give people the chance to hear directly from her why she supported this charity.

That was no different than any other charity she worked with back home. She took the time to study them and to get to know them, and she worked hard to be able to articulate why she supported the organizations that she chose to.

A few people stopped by and picked up brochures and signed the interest list. Anneliese tried to smile and to reassure them that there were great options to help get their lives, homes, businesses back on track.

"It feels like being home," she said to Matt during a lull in foot traffic.

"The soothing, temperate, air-conditioned climate of the Grand Provident reminds you of the tropical beaches of San Petro?"

For the second time today, she wanted to reach out and give him a playful swat. Maybe there was something about this island versus the one she normally called home.

She closed her eyes, and it came to her. Freedom.

Here, she felt free to be the person she'd always wanted to be, to not hold back because of what someone might think, because of protocol…because of fear that someone with a camera could jump out at any moment.

When she thought about it that way, what she'd just said to Matt was utterly wrong.

It didn't feel like home at all.

She waved a hand, in the air, figuratively clearing what she had intended to say.

"No, really, Annie, what do you mean?"

Her head popped like a ball at the end of a rubber band. "Annie?"

Matt took the last swallow of his coffee. "Yeah. You basically said you don't want to be a stuffy princess. Anneliese is a stuffy princess name. You need a name that reflects the real you, the person you say you want to be. Simple, open, approachable—Annie. I think you're an Annie now."

"You can't just become someone else." She shook her head in disbelief.

"Why not? Celebrities do it all the time."

She couldn't believe that was his logic. "I'm not a celebrity. I'm a princess. I can't just do whatever I want to do because I want to do it."

Matt locked his gaze with hers. His eyes were a gunmetal gray with just enough blue dropped in the irises to make her think of the deep water back home. "You just think that because it's the way you've always thought. But you've got a chance to make some changes in your life. Don't let people put words in your mouth anymore, Anneliese. Don't let them force actions on you that you don't want to take. Don't go back to San Petro the same princess in a gilded cage you were when you came to Port Provident. You came here to fly. You can't soar if you don't first step out in faith. Let your wings hold you up and take you where you need to go."

On that note, Matt waved at someone as they walked by and left Anneliese at the table to collect her thoughts. She didn't want to let her mind admit what her heart was telling her: Matt was right.

She'd come here to make a difference, to learn.

But what if the difference she needed to make was actually in herself?

What if the lesson she needed to learn was actually about herself?

In her heart, a peculiar feeling surfaced, almost like a bruise. It wasn't a stinging blood loss like a cut, but it let her know there'd been a bump and she'd need to afford herself time and healing to truly take it all in.

Before she could let it settle too much, Pastor Marco Ruiz from *La Iglesia* and The Grace Space sat down at one of the guest chairs across the table from Anneliese.

"It's good to see you here today, Your Highness."

"Please just call me Anneliese…actually, you can call me Annie, if you'd like." She breathed out all the hesitations of the past and decided to embrace a future where she could be anyone she wanted to be.

"Well, okay…if you're sure." The pastor seemed unsure of being on a nickname basis with royalty.

Anneliese smiled. "You know, I haven't been this sure of something in a long time. Now, how can I help you, Pastor Ruiz?"

"Well, the truth is, Annie, I don't like asking for help for myself much. But I know I need to ask now. My house is extensively damaged, and I have so much going on at the church and with The

Grace Space that I know I don't have enough hours in the day to give my house the attention it deserves and still tend to the needs of my flock at *La Iglesia de la Luz del Mundo.* How can I sign up for consideration to receive a Helping Hands remodel?"

Anneliese gathered a few papers off the table and sat them in front of the pastor, then handed him a green pen with the Helping Hands Homes logo on it in white. "Fill out these papers and then give them back to me. There's a committee that makes the decisions on who is selected, but there is a section on the second page that gives you the opportunity to explain why you are interested in working with Helping Hands. Be sure and use that space to tell the committee what you just told me. Don't be shy. That's something I'm learning myself these days."

The pastor picked up the pen and began to fill in the general information blanks at the top of the page. "With all the practice you must have meeting people and talking to them, I can't imagine you'd be shy."

"You speak to people every Sunday—probably at more than one service—but do you ever find that you're a different person on Tuesday than say, you are on Sunday?"

"Oh, I see what you're saying," he said with a nod. "You're likely right. There is a public Marco and a private Marco. I do my best to be as honest as I can with each, though."

"I just wish I could be the same person. I think I've spent most of my life trying to be one Anneliese at the expense of the other."

Marco laid his pen and the papers down and looked directly at her. "Can I give you a word of advice?"

Who would turn down personal instruction from a pastor?

"Yes, please."

"Do you know Proverbs 31?" he asked.

"I know it's in the Bible. I don't think I know any verses specifically, though."

He pulled out his smartphone and swiped and tapped with his thumb, then laid it on the table between them where they could both easily see the screen. "Proverbs 31 is generally regarded as a chapter in praise of what makes a good woman, a righteous woman."

He scrolled down the screen with his thumb, then double-tapped to enlarge the text when he came to what he was looking for.

"There it is. There are lots of good verses in this chapter, but here's the one I specifically wanted to share with you."

Anneliese craned her neck down toward the small glowing rectangle.

"Verse eight says 'Speak up for those who cannot speak for themselves,' and this is echoed again in verse nine where it asks women of virtue to 'Speak up and judge fairly; defend the rights of the poor and needy'."

Anneliese's finger touched the screen and dragged down as she continued reading. "'She speaks with wisdom, and faithful instruction is on her tongue.' I like the sound of that."

"Yes," Marco said in agreement. "And the chapter goes on to say that this woman's children rise up and call her blessed—and her husband does also."

Anneliese wiggled the fingers of her left hand. "No children, no husband. I only have a self-centered ex-fiancé and a childish younger brother."

Marco patted her hand when she laid it back on the table. "Ah, but someday, my dear. And until then, there are those who depend on you. But they depend on your honesty. Be wise and speak up. Be the woman you know you are in your heart. Be the one you that only you can be. Be who you were created to be—not just who you were born to be."

As he said that last sentence, the nagging soreness that she'd attributed to that bruise on her heart subsided. It made perfect sense.

"I was born to be a princess, but I need to figure out how to be Anneliese."

"Or Annie, if you prefer." He smiled knowingly. Anneliese couldn't confirm for sure, but she thought she saw him give her a quick wink.

Annie would speak up. She would speak truth. It was time to discover who Annie was.

~

"So it's just you doing the interview today, Matt?"

Jennifer Parker from the *Port Provident Herald* sat down at a table in the corner of the makeshift café at the back of the ballroom. She flipped open her laptop and laid her smartphone on the table and fiddled with a few buttons.

"Yeah. Anneliese de Cotriaro is here working the table with me today, but she didn't want to be included in the interview. She doesn't want things to be about her."

Jennifer cracked open a can of soda. "Too bad. She gives your story a really nice human interest side. And besides, I've met a lot of people in this job, but never a princess."

Matt leaned back in the wobbly folding chair. "Well, I think you just hit the nail on the head with that, though. She's not here to be a princess. She's here to help."

"I understand. Royalty relief makes a great story angle. The fact that a princess from another country would choose to come to Port Provident and help is a very compelling story to me."

"Well, as you probably know, there are ties between San Pedro and Port Provident, so it's not as random as it may seem at first glance." Anneliese walked behind Jennifer Parker, practically without a sound. Matt hadn't even noticed her approach. "Is this seat taken?"

"Absolutely not, Anneliese," Matt said, pushing the chair next to him back slightly.

She extended a hand across the table to the reporter. "Anneliese de Cotriaro. But you're welcome to call me Annie."

Others may have seen the smile she flashed as part of her greeting, but Matt knew it was meant only for him.

He felt a warmth like the gentle fall of a single sunbeam through a window take over his body, from his head to his toes. He didn't know what had happened in the fifteen minutes since he left the Helping Hands Homes table, but he knew he was grateful.

Anneliese de Cotriaro was capable of anything she wanted to accomplish. She was smart, compassionate, willing to work, and approachable. She could change any corner of the world she wanted to —she just had to be willing to step into her destiny instead of letting it hold her back.

Matt studied her as the thoughts tripped over themselves in his mind.

Oh, and she was beautiful.

Matt was afraid she was already making her mark on one very specific corner of the world—his heart.

With the introductions finished, Jennifer launched into a series of questions about the involvement of the sister cities prior to Hurricane Hope.

"Technology has made the sister city program a real partnership. Our school children in Rosada video chat once a month with school children here in Port Provident. I especially love what the fifth-grade classes have done—they've selected a book together and use their chat time to host a book club. It's a wonderful way to exchange perspectives and ideas and come together through the shared experience of reading."

"So your being here is more than just a one-off visit?"

"Absolutely. I came here with a purpose—to see where I could help Port Provident." Anneliese smoothed her hair back over the crown of her head. "But like our school children, I also came to learn. San Petro is an island too. And while we've been blessed to have dodged all the major hurricanes in our area for the recent past, I believe we have to be realistic. It's not a matter of *if*, but *when*, we take a blow from a hurricane. And I want to use the best practices I see here in Port Provident to better prepare San Petro and more efficiently recover when that day does come. I think that's what a real leader does."

Jennifer scribbled a few notes. "Now, you're not the official leader of San Petro, though, are you?"

Matt studied Anneliese's body language carefully. How she answered this would be very telling.

"No, I am not. I am second in line to the throne. My father is on the throne currently. However, after a stroke, much of his role falls to my younger brother, Federico, who is the Crown Prince. In our order of succession, the oldest male leapfrogs everyone else, and then the others fall in line according to birth order. And then we have a democratically-elected Parliament."

"So your brother supports what you're doing here?"

"I'm not here in an official capacity, so my trip is not sanctioned by the royal family. But I don't understand why anyone would not support reaching out and helping others."

Matt thought she deflected beautifully. And she had a point—what kind of person *wouldn't* support her being here?

The conversation wound around to the things Anneliese had done and seen while on the island. She spoke of hanging the drywall in the Solares family's house and how much she was looking forward to being there when they received the keys back to their house. She expressed her pride at how the *La Iglesia de la Luz del Mundo* community had rallied to create The Grace Space in a short period of time, filling a need without wading through government red tape. She answered Jennifer's questions about her time with the two former presidents and how she expected their foundation to pave a path to progress for many groups in the city who were trying to help residents.

"What about the remainder of your time here? What are you looking forward to before you go back home?" Jennifer adjusted the position of her recorder to better capture Anneliese's response.

"I got a voicemail this morning that next Friday night, I've been invited to attend a fundraiser gala in Houston with the Foster/George Gulf Coast Recovery Fund. I haven't had a chance to call and give my answer yet, but I am looking to being there and being a part of a memorable evening that will do very much good. I think it's a wonderful way to bridge being Princess Anneliese of San Petro and Annie de Cotriaro, a person who wants to do the most good she can for a place she feels a special bond with."

Matt's hand had been resting under the table in his lap. At her statement, he cautiously lifted it and placed it on top of Anneliese's knee, then gave a gentle squeeze. It wasn't just an acknowledgment of pride in the words she'd said or the confidence with which she'd said them. It was his way of wanting to hold on to the moment, to this woman, in any way he could.

He knew she'd be gone soon—she'd just confirmed that with Jennifer. There was no way he could act on that feeling like sunshine in his soul. It was only strengthening the longer he listened to the passion in this remarkable woman's voice, but that was light that he'd just have to find a way to hide.

Matt was a guy who was used to making things happen, building things from the ground up.

It frustrated him to know there wasn't a thing he could do here, except leave his hand lightly on her knee for as long as she'd let him—and be grateful for every moment.

"Come on." Matt reached for Anneliese's hand when she opened the door to her hotel room.

"Come where?" She gave the doorway a serious look, not moving to cross it. "I don't even have any makeup on. I was starting to get ready for bed."

He reached for her hand again, and this time, he caught it. She didn't pull back but also didn't change the expression on her face.

"That's just going to have to wait." He tugged gently on her fingers. "My favorite place in Port Provident has reopened—and you're coming with me."

"Matt." She turned his name into an extended number of syllables, each one licked with a gentle Spanish accent. "Look at me. I can't go out like this."

"You really think anyone is going to see you? It's dark. And this is a place only locals know. And there are barely any locals on the island right now. Port Provident's population is primarily made up of contractors, insurance adjusters, and FEMA employees."

"Do you promise no one is going to see me?" She peered out from around the edge of the door and snuck a quick glance in each direction down the hallway.

"Annie, I'm barely going to be able to see you. It's dark outside." He stepped closer and leaned over her ear as he lowered his voice. "Can you trust me?"

She let out a sigh. "Okay. Let me get some decent shoes on."

As they walked down to the parking lot where his truck was parked, Anneliese scraped her hair back into a rough ponytail and fidgeted with the hem of her bright pink running-style shorts. Matt couldn't tell her how adorable she looked. She'd never believe him.

He kept the talk very small as he drove to the western tip of Provident Island. He could tell she still didn't understand exactly what was up his sleeve.

"So where are we headed?"

"The edge of the earth." Matt smiled broadly at her as he put on the brake at the last stoplight they'd encounter on the island in this direction.

"We have a place like that on San Petro, too. The coastline along much of the back side of the island is very rocky, and because of that, the land out there is fairly undeveloped. All the tourist development is on the side of the island that faces the border coastline between Mexico and Belize. That's where the beaches and the reefs are. But sometimes, I like to go out to the back of the island and listen to the crash of the waves against the rocks. I feel like it centers me."

"So you'll understand exactly how I feel about this place."

"What makes it so special?" Her head was turned to look out the window and take in the landscape of Provident Island as they drove.

It certainly wasn't as clean as he was used to out here—debris sucked out of garages and off of boats still littered the sides of the road. Fences were down. Seagrass and plastic bags were stuck in every nook and cranny.

Still, just being on this far stretch of the highway out to a place he'd been fascinated by since he was a kid did his soul good. He couldn't wait to see how it had fared.

Matt angled his truck toward a short road that was now more dirt than the gravel-paved it had once been. He bumped the truck over a curb and pulled up on the grass, then parked at the base of the Point Provident Lighthouse.

He put the truck in park and pulled his gaze from the ground to the light on top. The old girl looked stellar, all things considered. Her red and white stripes still circled the strong tower, and none of her windows seemed to be blown out.

"This is the Point Provident Lighthouse."

Anneliese tilted her head so she could see all the way up to the top. "Wow, gorgeous."

Matt got out of the cab of the truck and walked around to open Anneliese's door. Then he grabbed a dusty quilted blanket out of the bed of his truck. He used it to keep things he was transporting from messing up other items or the bed of the truck. But for tonight, it would have a different use.

He wanted to give Anneliese as much of the world—his world—as he could while she was here. If he couldn't hope to move forward, couldn't hope to have her for his own forever, he could at least hope to create memories that neither of them would ever forget.

"She's been the symbol of Port Provident for generations. My great-grandfather, John Peoples, came here after the Great Storm of 1915 destroyed Port Provident. He went up to the top and fixed the lighthouse so that they could signal the ships that were stuck out in the water. There were some that limped through the storm, and they needed help. He was a hero."

Matt cupped his hand behind Anneliese's elbow and guided her through the grass. He spread out the blanket and gestured for her to join him to sit on it.

"It sounds like it. We had a hurricane come through in 1915 as well. I wonder if it was the same one." She gently lowered herself down on the faded quilted blanket.

"September 13, 1915." Matt knew the date like it was a milestone in his own life—every native of Port Provident did. The stories had been passed down for generations and had become a part of the framework of their town and their lives.

"Ours was September 8, 1915. I bet it was the same storm. How amazing that your history and my history have that connection. Your great-grandfather played a role in saving your town after it and mine played a role in saving Rosada and San Petro. That's the kind of leader I think we deserve in San Petro. Federico just isn't that kind of person."

Matt leaned back on his elbows and stretched out. "What do you mean? You've mentioned him before, and it hasn't been particularly flattering, but you haven't really said much about him."

Anneliese surveyed Matt's relaxed posture and lowered herself to a similar position. "He's concerned more about appearances than people. We've been an independent nation since the late 1700s when we negotiated a treaty with Spain. And before that, even, we had a proud history. We have natural resources and a tropical climate. There's so much to love about San Petro and so many industries we could grow to help our people thrive. But Federico is only concerned about tourism because looking good and having a good time are all that matter to him. He'd like to see us be the Caribbean version of Monte Carlo. I'd like to see us provide opportunity and growth to our people and be a small country that people of many countries and many walks of life respect and admire."

"There's no mistaking the conviction in your voice. I believe you can do just that. I've seen the way you've worked here—how you've gone seamlessly from a construction site to charming two men who were the so-called leaders of the free world. I don't think there's anything you *can't* do, Annie."

She sighed heavily. "I can't be queen. I can't get out of Federico's shadow."

"What about the vote?"

"I have to keep the faith. But I feel very far away from it being here. I only know what I'm being told, which isn't much."

"But you have people supporting you, right?" Matt couldn't imagine anyone not wanting to throw their support behind this woman who cared so deeply about her country that she would come to America just to find out how to make things at home better. "You should be bold about your vision and get more San Petrans on board."

"I do. Several of them, in fact. My secretary has been sending me updates. I'm choosing to keep a low profile though. I can't be seen as meddling in the affairs of state. I lose all credibility with my people—and myself—if it even remotely looks like I'm staging some kind of coup d'état."

Matt let her words sink in as he looked up at the stars. "That makes perfect sense."

"It's actually nice to have slipped away to Port Provident and to be away from it all. That way, if anyone does ask me, I can honestly say I've been far away from all the dealings."

"A wise strategy." Matt rolled onto his right side, facing Anneliese, and propped his head up on one hand. "The moonlight suits you, you know."

A shy smile feathered across her lips. "What are you talking about?"

"You. I'm talking about you. You don't like to talk about yourself or take credit for the things you do. But I can."

"No, you can't." She met his eyes with a piercing gaze.

"Try and stop me." Matt threw down the challenge like a gauntlet in a royal courtyard of old.

Anneliese raised herself to a sitting position and placed one hand over his mouth, shushing him.

Matt swung his top arm around and circled her waist, then pulled her down playfully, knocking her off balance and making her remove her hand. He didn't let go but instead kept the gentle, pulling pressure of his forearm around her hips.

Within a moment, only inches separated them.

The moonlight in her hair that had made him do a double-take only a minute before now fell fully across her face. The sound of the waves crashing on the rocks below the small cliff on which the lighthouse stood drowned out everything but the thought of her—his beautiful Annie.

Matt stretched his head upward and met her lips with his own, then slid his now-free support arm behind her head, keeping her close. She wrapped an arm around his shoulder, and it triggered a need in him to deepen the kiss, to build that memory of taste and smell and touch before she went back to San Petro and was lost to him forever.

A cloud shifted in front of the moon, cutting in half the shine that had fallen on them. Matt took it as a sign to make a shift himself.

Anneliese didn't say anything. Matt tried to decipher her mood, but she'd been raised to conceal her thoughts, and she was using her training to her advantage right now.

"Anneliese—" Matt started to speak, although he didn't quite know what to say.

She raised her hand once again and laid two fingers lightly on his lips. The contact with her skin made them tingle with the most recent of memories.

"Annie. Call me Annie."

The shy smile on her face sparkled like the shimmer of the moon's glow where it touched the water. Matt had been coming to Provident Point and visiting this lighthouse most of his life. But he'd never felt peace in his soul like this until a hurricane blew a blonde-haired, spirited princess into his life.

Someone had brought three bouquets of green-and-white balloons and staggered them along the length of the Solares' front porch. Anneliese stood off to the left of the middle grouping and leaned around one of the helium-filled spheres to catch a brief glimpse of Matt.

He stood next to Mrs. Solares, and Anneliese's stomach did a backflip when he casually put his arm around the woman's shoulder and leaned down to say something to her.

Anneliese knew he was sharing some word of encouragement, not the same types of things he shared with her in the shadow of the lighthouse. But the simple gesture took her mind back to Provident Point—and thoughts about how she never wanted to leave this place.

She loved the freedom she'd found here. She loved the voice she was growing into—she was taking Pastor Ruiz's lesson to heart and speaking up with confidence. She loved being a part of a community concerned for the well-being of others, a place with a can-do spirit.

But most of all, as she snuck another look around the balloons, she loved the time she spent with Matt. In fact, if she chose to be honest with herself, she'd say she was falling in love with Matt—even if that was a ridiculous notion.

Her heart had never embraced feelings like this before. She'd never allowed herself to go in that direction. She'd always believed she wasn't meant to date like other people did, but instead would be paired off in an arrangement that was more business than fairy tale.

And indeed, everything about her time with Rafael had been just that—an exercise in checking boxes until they got to the altar to check the final box. Her relationship with him had only been about duty.

But the time she'd spent with Matt was different than any time she'd spent with anyone, ever. He took the time to explain things to her. He valued her opinion. He clearly wanted what was best for her and took the time to hear her out and offer his own thoughts in return.

She also noticed him like she'd never noticed any other man. She couldn't quit giving a slight bend forward from her waist, just to look past the green and white balloons. Today, he wore a collared knit shirt in a dark forest green with the Helping Hands Homes logo embroidered on the chest in white thread. He had a pair of khaki slacks on and shiny brown dress shoes. His hair spiked up just a little bit in front, and the grin he wore on his face was relaxed. She knew it would circle through her mind for days.

David Long joined the group assembled on the porch by leaping over the three steps from the sidewalk.

"It's time to celebrate!" David jingled a set of keys between two fingers. "This is a milestone day."

A group of Port Provident's most well-known people had gathered on the lawn, including City Councilwoman Angela Ruiz and her nephew, Pastor Marco Ruiz, who was the Solares family's pastor at *La Iglesia*. The volunteers from Dynacrude, the Houston-based oil company that had pitched in to make the rebuild possible, stood in a group off to the left. Three TV cameras had staked out spots near the curb, and Anneliese also spotted Jennifer Parker from the *Port Provident Herald* and her photographer.

All in all, it was a meaningful and robust crowd. Anneliese's heart swelled with pride to be a part of it.

Dave gave a few brief remarks, then turned the microphone over to Matt.

"I'm not really one for public speaking—I'm more of a guy who conveys things through craftsmanship. But Port Provident is my hometown, and kicking off this one hundred homes project has been special. I want to thank the Solares family for their partnership in turning over the keys and letting us stir up a whirlwind of activity to replace what the hurricane stole away. The Dynacrude team has worked tirelessly and supported us with funds."

Matt stopped for a moment and looked around the porch, then stretched out the cord on the microphone as he walked over to where Anneliese stood.

"And along the way, we had a special visitor from Port Provident's sister city of Rosada, San Petro. Anneliese de Cotriaro mucked out a broken refrigerator, pulled out cabinets, hung drywall—everything I asked of my crew and volunteers, she took on as well. And she helped us secure the funds we needed to make this happen ninety-nine more times. Annie, you've been a fantastic partner in all of this—and I'd like for you to be the one who opens the door to welcome the Solares family home."

A respectful round of applause rose as Matt concluded his remarks. He patted Anneliese on the shoulder as she walked past.

Tears started to well up in her own eyes, and Anneliese mentally chastised herself. This wasn't her moment. This moment was for the Solares family.

But with just a few short sentences, Matt had spoken to her heart—and he probably didn't even know he'd done it.

"Bienvenido a su casa, la familia de Solares," Anneliese said as she carefully turned the knob. With just a little force, she opened the door fully and with more than just her Spanish-language words, welcomed the Solares family back to their home with actions.

As Mrs. Solares walked around her newly-restored home with a mixture of gasps and squeals of delight, Matt slipped in behind Anneliese and put his arm around her shoulder—just as she'd been dreaming about for the last ten minutes.

Lost in the joy surrounding the culmination of hard work, Anneliese leaned her head back into the tender gesture and let it rest at the edge of his chest.

"You seem just as happy as she is," Matt murmured near the top of Anneliese's head.

"How could I not be? This is changing the world, one life at a time." She tilted her head up and looked at Matt as the assembled guests swirled around them, taking in the completed home. "But I think it's my life that's changed the most."

6
——————

"You're coming with me Friday night to the fundraising dinner, aren't you?" Anneliese snuggled deeper into Matt's arms as they watched the last trickle of light drip from the sky behind the horizon. They brought their dinner to Point Provident almost every night now, and ate on the worn-out grey blanket under the shadow of the candy-cane styled lighthouse.

It had been a few days since the Solares family's homecoming, and work was now well underway at the next house on the Helping Hands Homes list. Matt spent his days tearing out fixtures, hammering in nails, and dreaming about the end of the day when he could drive with Anneliese to the easternmost point on the island, take in the sunset, and make wishes on stars about never having to give nights like these up.

Matt knew that wish could never come true, though. This would be Anneliese's last weekend before returning to San Petro.

He couldn't decide if he wanted to make the most of it or live in denial that the sands were slipping through their hourglass.

"I wasn't invited, actually. And I don't have a tuxedo or anything to wear. I didn't bring my formal clothes to hang in the hotel closet while I rebuilt one hundred homes. Anything that would fit the bill for me to wear is back in Austin."

72

She laid a hand softly on his chest as a gulf breeze ruffled through her hair. "I get to bring a guest. I'll take care of everything. Just be in the lobby of the Crockett Court Hotel at four o'clock Friday afternoon."

"What are you, my fairy godmother?"

"No, silly." She turned over and faced him with a grin that would have made Gus-Gus, the mouse from *Cinderella*, proud. "I'm a princess. But I do have a trick or two up my sleeve."

"Is that sleeve full of glitter?" Matt wanted to tease her, to hold that smile on her face just a little longer.

"You'll have to meet me at the Crockett Court if you want to find out."

"You drive a hard bargain, Your Royal Highness."

She nodded. "I've learned about speaking up, remember?"

As they'd eaten dinner tonight, she'd revealed the conversation she'd had with Marco Ruiz at the Port Provident Recovery Fair.

"I remember."

She snuggled back comfortably in his arms and swished a hand at the stars in the sky. "I am so glad I've been here for this."

"For the stars?" He had to admit, with the lighthouse not yet turned back on, this was one of the darkest corners of their little world. The stars glowed like a shake of powder across the sky.

She shook her head. "For it all. I'm going to miss this place when I go home. I'm going to miss the anonymity just to be Annie most of the time. I'll miss doing work that makes me tired but fulfilled at the end of the day. I'll miss coming here to Provident Point and listening to the waves with you."

He already knew the answer, but the question pushed out of Matt's mouth before he had the clarity of thought to stop it. "What if you don't leave? What if you stay here?"

"Matt, I can't. You know I can't. I have to go home—I can't be away any more than I have been, with the vote deadline looming. I've done what I set out to do here. Now it's time to go home and put those lessons—the personal ones as well as the working ones—into practice."

He didn't have anything to say in response. He should have kept his mouth shut. He would have kicked himself for letting himself sound desperate to keep her here by his side, but Annie's legs were draped over his own, and he would have disturbed her if he'd executed the roundhouse kick he wanted to.

"I will leave with one regret, though."

Matt's heart skipped a beat. Would her regret be about him? And what would he say in reply?

"I will have come all this way and still really not seen much of Texas."

His heart cynically laughed at itself for freezing with suspense. At last, he found the words to respond with. "What do you mean?"

"I told you that I've been fascinated by Texas history since I read that book as a child. Now, here I am, spending weeks in Texas—and I still won't see the Alamo or much more of the state than the sliver of Houston that I can see from the Crockett Court Hotel."

"Oh, I see." Matt heard the disappointment in her voice. At least he wasn't the only one feeling that way tonight—he just wished he'd been the reason for her change in tone, instead of Davy Crockett, Jim Bowie, and William B. Travis, the heroes of the Alamo. "And you're sure you couldn't extend your visit so you could take a road trip?"

"No, I can't. The date for the vote is set. I need to get back home so I can speak up as I've committed myself to doing." She scooted out of the protection of his arms and over to a spot on the blanket at his side. "Besides, I already told you, I can't drive."

"I remember."

She sat on her heels, legs folded underneath her. She wore jeans and a casual long-sleeved lightweight gray sweater with a neckline that reminded Matt of the soft curves at the top of a heart shape.

"I promise I won't forget, Matt."

He couldn't take his eyes off the buttons that closed the top of her blouse. "Forget what?"

"This." She leaned forward and cupped his chin with both her hands, pulling him into a kiss that contained all the power of the constellations twinkling over their heads.

Matt pulled her tight and pulled everything into the kiss. If she promised she wasn't going to forget, he would make sure she had something worth remembering.

He held a part back from the kiss, the part where he still scolded himself for ever hoping that maybe she could stay just a little longer.

Matt knew how this fairy tale ended. He'd go to the ball with Cinderella. Then the clock would strike midnight and her last weekend in America would be over, and she'd go back to her home and the people who depended upon her.

He knew he'd buy the gossip magazines to keep up with her for a while—just long enough for him to teach himself that there'd never been any hope for a long-term love between a work boot-wearing Texan and a woman in whose world a blue collar meant a priceless sapphire necklace.

Matt generally thought of himself as good at following directions. It was an imperative on a construction site, because the easiest way to get yourself or someone else hurt was to disregard instructions. At four o'clock on Friday, he arrived at the Crockett Court Hotel, one of the finest, newest luxury hotels in downtown Houston. He'd done what he was told, but he didn't know why he was here or even what he was looking for.

He walked around the lobby, looking up at the giant, colorful Chihuly-style glass chandelier that dominated the main entry. It made him feel very small—and actually a little bit boring.

"*Señor* McGregor?" A man with a heavy Spanish accent came toward him.

"Yes?" Matt felt like he was in a spy movie where everyone knew him, but he didn't know anything about his situation.

"I am Carlos Pampalón, private secretary to Her Royal Highness Princess Anneliese of San Petro."

Now Matt knew he'd entered the twilight zone.

"Please come with me." Carlos beckoned with one hand as he

turned and walked toward the bank of elevators at the back of the lobby. "I have everything ready in your room upstairs."

"I don't have a room upstairs." Matt waited for the man to say that he wasn't a royal private secretary—he was just some actor hired for a few hours to play a practical joke.

"Everything is taken care of for you, sir. Her Royal Highness had me fly in to Houston to ensure that this evening comes together flawlessly and meets her standards."

Matt watched out of the glass-backed elevator. The floors whizzed past as he and Carlos ascended to…well, to wherever they were going. As he contemplated the blur of floors and shrinking objects and people below him, Matt tried to reconcile in his mind the Annie in his arms at the base of the lighthouse with Her Royal Highness Princess Anneliese who apparently just had to snap her fingers and have staff at her beck and call—even in foreign countries.

They got off the elevator and Matt followed Carlos' footsteps down the red-carpeted hallway, then left, then right, then left again until they came to a pair of double doors made of a dark-stained wood. Carlos took a keycard out of his pocket and swiped it in the slot. He pushed open the doors and then stood to the side to let Matt walk through first.

"Please come in, *Señor* McGregor."

Matt hadn't exactly had a shabby upbringing, and he'd seen quite a bit of the world, but as he walked through the doors, he felt a push like a backdraft.

He was literally blown away.

Instinctively, he let out a low whistle, then caught himself when he realized Carlos had heard his sound of shocked appreciation.

"This meets with your approval?" Anneliese's most trusted advisor asked.

"I think it will work, Mr. Pampalón." Matt took in the thick, plush rugs, the ornate furniture upholstered in heavy silk and trimmed with gold-accented wood. He couldn't imagine whose approval this *wouldn't* meet. "But I still don't understand what all this is about."

"This is the Presidential Suite. Her Royal Highness is one floor above us in the Royal Suite." Carlos pointed toward a set of closed doors. "Her Royal Highness wanted to ensure that everything was perfect for the ball this evening and called me to come with a few members of her staff from home. She mentioned you did not have a tuxedo with you. Through those doors is your private room. I've brought a stylist and several suits to choose from. Then Joio will take care of your hair and any other last-minute details. While you're being attended to, I'll call room service for some refreshments for you."

Matt's mind sloshed around like water in a goldfish bowl. "I don't even know what to say."

"Nothing is necessary sir, other than telling Hector what size suit and shoes you require. He's waiting for you in there."

Matt decided this whole display of luxury really was happening—and to question or protest any further wouldn't make any sense of it. There wasn't any sense to be made of it.

So, he decided to make the most of it.

He would find out what would happen if the glass slipper was actually a wingtip. He would find out what it would be like if the fairy tale was backwards and Prince Charming was instead the one who had ridden in a pumpkin carriage that night to meet Cinderella.

The tuxedo fit expertly. A tailor had made minor last-minute adjustments, but the moment Matt put the high-end designer garment on, he didn't think there was much to improve on how the finely-woven fabric felt as good as a second skin. The hairstylist gave his hair a small trim and then used a lightweight gel to fix everything in place —it wasn't too trendy, but it still appeared fresh with a little edge.

Matt could honestly say he'd never looked better in his life.

"*Señor* McGregor, it is time to go downstairs to the event." Carlos called Matt away from the giant plate-glass window where he'd been reflecting on the Houston skyline.

"What about Anneliese?" He stopped and corrected himself. Everything about this late afternoon had been formal, polished. "I mean, Her Royal Highness."

"The princess has requested that you meet her in the sitting room adjacent to the Royal Suite and then you both can go to the ballroom together."

Carlos opened the doors to the Presidential Suite for Matt, then closed them softly. "This way, sir."

Once in the elevator, Carlos swiped his card and punched the button labeled "RS." There would be no getting to Anneliese without strict security.

Carlos held open the elevator doors, and Matt stepped through, still trying to get used to the formality.

"It is the single door to the left of the large double doors, *Señor* McGregor. You may go ahead. I will wait for the two of you to come back to the elevator."

Matt walked up to the door, then hesitated for a moment.

He knew what he'd gone through to get ready since Carlos Pampalon had met him under the colorful corkscrews of Chihuly glass. He couldn't imagine what Anneliese's day had been like. He hadn't seen her all day. She wasn't at the job site this morning, so all he could assume was that she'd been here at the Crockett Court, holed up with her personally-selected team that had flown in from a small jewel in the Caribbean to wait hand-and-foot on their princess.

Anneliese might like the freedom and anonymity that she had on the streets of Port Provident, but Matt knew in the pit of his stomach that this was the world she was accustomed to.

This was who she was.

He might think of her as his Annie under the moonlight at the lighthouse. But that just wasn't reality. The reality was that she was indeed Her Royal Highness Princess Anneliese of San Petro.

All the drywall and nails in the world couldn't change that.

Matt rolled his hand into a fist and knocked on the door, both dying to see Anneliese and scared to death that once he did, it would change everything once and for all. Once he saw her fully made up as Princess Anneliese, he didn't think he'd ever be able to think of her as just Annie again.

The door swung open. Matt didn't see anyone pulling it back. In fact, all he saw was the incredible, expansive living area of the Royal Suite.

"Matt? Is that you?"

Anneliese's voice carried through the rooms.

"It is. Carlos is out in the hallway. He'll meet us at the elevator."

"Perfect. I'm almost finished. Why don't you come back here? Turn right, then right again."

A maid stepped out from behind the door and dipped formally to Matt as he walked through. His mind was a bit blown. No one had ever bowed or bobbed or curtseyed—or whatever it was that she did—to him before.

He followed Anneliese's directions through the ultimate penthouse suite.

And then he stopped.

More breathtaking than the Chihuly, more elegant than the gilded furniture, more royal than all the formality he'd experienced this afternoon—that was Anneliese.

She stood on a short pedestal in front of a three-way mirror as a woman in all black made adjustments to the tiny train at the back of her heavy green satin skirt. Deep pleats encircled her waist, making it appear tinier and curvier than ever. The dress was strapless and free of embellishment. Around her neck, she wore a necklace of nine square-cut green stones, each ringed with a frame of tiny slivers of diamonds that looked like a wreath of icicles. Matching three-stone earrings dropped from each delicate earlobe. She wore a heavy bracelet of the same stones.

On top of the same blonde hair he'd watched her scrape back into a ponytail ten times a day while they worked alongside each other now sat a delicate tiara, all diamonds and dew-dropped accents of green stones. One large square green stone rose above the rest of the chips of ice and moss.

"Anneliese…you look incredible."

He felt so inadequate bestowing that compliment. It didn't do justice to anything about her appearance.

"It's probably a bit much. But this is my favorite dress and parure. I figured that since both presidents will be there and it's black-tie, I could get away with it. I find that Americans tend to be disappointed if you don't look like what they think a princess should look like at formal events. And just for tonight, I'd like to use this tiara for good and raise as much money for the presidential fund as I can so that more funds come to Helping Hands Homes."

"Well, they've already told us the amount that the grant is for, so I think it's wonderful that you want to raise more money, but it won't affect us at Helping Hands."

Anneliese delicately stepped off the tailor's platform. "Yes, it will. That's a condition of my appearing here tonight. Twenty-five percent of funds raised for Port Provident tonight will go straight to Helping Hands."

A lump formed in Matt's throat. "I don't know what to say," he practically croaked out the words.

She swung her arms out and took his hands in hers, then stood back to fully appreciate his own fancy dress transformation.

"I don't want you to say anything. It was one of those opportunities where if I took that verse from Proverbs 31 and I spoke up, I could do more good for something that I care deeply about—and someone I care deeply for. I can use who I am to make a difference."

"Whether you realize it or not, Anneliese, since the moment you set foot on Port Provident, you've been making a difference."

She pulled a hand out of Matt's grasp and pressed the pad of one cool finger against the newly-exfoliated skin of his lips. "*Sssh.* And I thought I'd already told you once—when it's just you and me, the name's Annie."

Anneliese had stood in many ballrooms, swished many skirts, worn many tiaras. But she'd never felt a rush like she did when she entered Grand Ballroom A at the Crockett Court Hotel. She knew she had to focus ahead, had to look like a princess, had to make the right eye contact with the right people.

But she didn't want to. All she wanted to do was look at Matt in his perfectly-tailored tuxedo.

She compromised with herself by threading her arm around his and keeping the palm of her hand curved around the swell of muscle in the middle of his forearm.

A constant crackle of electricity flowed between them. In a room where the champagne and fine wine would be flowing freely tonight among the donors and esteemed guests, Anneliese decided that the single most intoxicating thing was the connection between her and Matt.

Both presidents singled her out for conversation and made introductions between her and some of the elites who had been invited to take part in this special night. She and Matt each shared their stories of the Hundred Homes Project and of the mission of Helping Hands Homes. They each answered numerous questions about the state of Port Provident from people who had seen the scenes on the news, but obviously were not traveling to the island themselves.

After more than an hour, it felt like they'd been face-to-face with almost everyone in the room. The evening's emcee asked everyone to take their seats, and shortly thereafter, former President George stepped behind the podium at the front of the room.

He started with a joke, and the crowd laughed at his usual self-deprecating wit.

Then, he began to talk about Anneliese and her work with Helping Hands Homes.

"It's not every day you see someone who never has to get their hands dirty take a plane to another country to help those in need. Port Provident is a sister city to San Petro's capital of Rosada, but never has a city had a sibling so willing to share and give. Her time here is almost finished, but when President Foster and I unexpectedly saw her at the Solares house restoration recently, we knew that we needed to change the focus of this fundraiser. We wanted to invite her here tonight so that you could see for yourself what she's done and that we could all honor her work in the Port Provident community in the best way we all know how—by donating more money to the Foster/George

Gulf Coast Recovery Fund so that we all can keep up the good work that's been started here, even after Princess Anneliese goes home."

The audience broke into a round of applause that did not die down.

Slowly, Anneliese rose from her seat and gave the crowd a quick wave and a smile. She felt the heat of a small blush spread over her cheeks.

She had not expected such a heartfelt tribute tonight and was genuinely touched by the reception both for the work she had done and for herself as a person.

"Princess Anneliese, I would like to present you with the Difference Maker Award from the Foster/George Gulf Coast Recovery Fund." President George took a walnut-colored plaque from President Foster's hands and held it up over the microphone. "Please come up here and accept this award and our sincere thanks on behalf of all of those here in the Gulf Coast area who are recovering from this life-changing event."

She nodded and pushed her chair back a little further so she could make her way to the front from her table at the middle of the room. When she reached President George, he enveloped her in a hug before handing over the plaque. President Foster stood and did the same.

Then they both stood away from the microphone and gestured for Anneliese to step forward.

"I hadn't planned any remarks for tonight, and I certainly hadn't planned on receiving an award. I came tonight because like you, I believe in the people of Port Provident and I want to take whatever opportunities I have to help make their path to recovery a little more straight."

Anneliese's eyes locked on Matt's in the audience, and at once, she knew what she wanted to say. She would speak up.

"I came to Port Provident both to help the citizens of my sister city and to learn what we in San Petro can do in the event of our next hurricane strike. I came for the people of Port Provident today and the people of San Petro tomorrow. But I couldn't have achieved my goals without someone very special—Matt McGregor, the director of the Helping Hands Homes Southern Region, is here with me tonight. He could have said he didn't need the distraction of someone like me on his project—well, maybe he did, but he didn't say it to me. Instead, he taught me what I needed to know and ensured that my time here not only benefited the project we were working on, but would benefit my country when I went home. He's already hard at work on the second remodel for Helping Hands Homes and will not stop until he reaches his goal of one hundred homes by Christmas. He also taught me that true friendship is about finding that '*a ha*' moment of commonality between two people. I know we all have something in common because we're all here to support a good cause tonight. I encourage you to have your own '*a ha*' moment and think about how you can best support Port Provident's recovery. Thank you again from the bottom of my heart—it has been a pleasure to be here in Texas and lend my support."

Anneliese brought her plaque back with her and quickly laid it on the table so her hands were free to once again wrap around Matt's arm. Soon, the multiple courses of dinner were finished and the evening's emcee announced that the band would begin playing shortly and he hoped everyone would enjoy the rest of the evening on the dance floor.

Matt hadn't said much during the meal. He'd sat quietly, carefully studying the faces at each table. Plenty of people had wanted to talk to Anneliese, so she hadn't lacked for conversation.

Finally, he looked at her. His gaze was earnest. His eyes looked almost like the color of flint. "Shall we?" he said simply.

"Shall we what?" Anneliese asked in return—she thought he wanted to dance, but she wasn't entirely sure and needed to clarify.

"Dance. This is my moment with Cinderella at the ball."

"What happens at midnight?" Anneliese had visions of mice scrambling across the room and the elegantly set tables popping into pumpkins.

"I don't know. But I plan to find out." He whispered low so that no one else around them could hear. A tingle shot down her spine. It felt like the whisper of snowflakes.

He stood up, pulled her chair out and helped her stand. She'd taken dancing lessons since she was young. Never had Anneliese been nervous about stepping onto a floor to dance. She was trained in classical and current styles, and she had always felt confident in her skills.

Until this very moment. The snowflake pitter and patter through the center of her back and the shallow breaths that refused to sink all the way into her lungs made her acutely aware that this would be no ordinary dance.

Matt led her to a place at the far corner of the dance floor.

The leader of the band spoke into his microphone as the rest of his colleagues readied themselves to begin with a strum and a hum.

"We'll play a variety of music tonight, so I know all of you will hear at least one of your favorites, no matter what your style is. But we always like to start with one special song—the traditional Anne Murray and *Could I Have This Dance?*"

The band broke into soft country strains. Matt pulled her close and reflexively, Anneliese's eyes closed. Although the band leader seemed to indicate that this was a well-known song, Anneliese had never heard it before. But as they rolled into the chorus, Anneliese took the words to heart, and a solitary tear slipped from her left eye.

"Princesses don't cry," Matt said as he twirled her around.

She mustered a half-smile. She couldn't let the room full of people she'd just asked for donations of their time and money see her losing herself like this.

"They do when they realize all they want is what's in the song and they can't have it."

"What do you want?"

His face was only inches from hers. The closeness made her remember every second of every kiss they'd shared. She swallowed hard, determined to fight against the emotions pushing up from her heart and into her throat and eyes and mind.

She couldn't tell him what she wanted to say to him. She couldn't even tell herself the honest answer—she wanted to dance with him for the rest of her life. "I want to go out to the patio. I need some fresh air."

Matt straightened and put his palm on the small of her back, guiding her out the larger-than-life floor-to-ceiling glass doors. The night air tasted crisp like fall, and she gulped the cool air as far into her lungs as she could.

"Now, that's not like you, Annie. Can you tell me what's wrong?"

At the sound of his baritone voice calling her Annie, she felt the tension in her shoulders flatten and relax.

But she still couldn't just come right out and say the words rolling around in her head. She just couldn't. It wasn't fair. Her heart told her it wasn't just about wanting to dance with someone special for the rest of her life, it was about extending the moment—living in it, making time stand still.

She could tell him that.

"I don't want this to end. I can see Houston out there." She pointed at the twinkle and burn of the millions of lights that made up the skyline of one of the largest cities in America. "But there's so much else out there. And I'm going to miss it."

Matt stood behind her and tucked a finger underneath the uppermost stone on her necklace. His heat contrasted with the cool stone. "No, you're not."

She twisted her head just enough that she could see the profile of his face in the night shadows around them on the terrace. The accent diamonds on her necklace grazed her skin.

"I don't understand."

"If we leave now, can you work some of that Cinderella magic and have your Fairy Godfather Carlos arrange hotel rooms and clothes and toothbrushes in San Antonio?"

Anneliese turned all the way around and slid her palms up the lapels of Matt's tuxedo. "I don't know if I could just leave all these people, Matt."

"You have two choices, my dear. Stay here and be Princess Anneliese and do exactly what you're supposed to for the rest of your days. Or this one last time, be Annie. See the things you've dreamed of seeing. Be the person your heart wants you to be. Be bold."

Anneliese bit her lip. She wanted to say yes so badly. Years and years of training and rules and etiquette pulled at her like thick rope.

"Annie…I can't hear your answer. Speak up."

She'd promised herself in the cavernous room at the Grand Provident that she would not stay silent and in the corner anymore. Even if she had to put on the mask of Princess Anneliese, she would keep the spirit of Annie de Cotriaro inside her, glowing like an eternal flame.

Annie would speak up.

And in Annie de Cotriaro, Her Royal Highness Princess Anneliese found her voice.

"I'll make the call. Let's go."

Matt leaned his head down, and Anneliese pulled her hands further up his lapels, and brought them together, locked behind his neck.

Everything *was* bigger in Texas. Even the kisses.

7

———

Carlos was as magical as any fairy tale guardian. By the time Matt and Anneliese pulled into San Antonio, they had two rooms at the Alamo Garden Hotel on San Antonio's historic Riverwalk and several days' worth of clothes, shoes, and other necessities in the closets.

"Look there—he's even got a toothbrush next to the sink." Matt pointed at a small collection of toiletries on the bathroom counter in his room. "And it's red, my favorite color. How did he know?"

Anneliese smiled brightly, a complete one-hundred-and-eighty-degree turn from her earlier trepidation on the dance floor back in Houston. "I don't know how he knows. I don't know how he does it. He just does. He picks up the phone, and things happen."

"Well, I plan to make things happen too, Annie. I'm not going to let Carlos out-do me. But all that starts tomorrow. Your room is right next door. Here's your key." Matt handed her the credit card-sized rectangle of plastic. "I'll be at your door at eight o'clock tomorrow morning. We'll have breakfast together, then in true Carlos fashion, I am going to make Texas history come alive for you."

She leaned tenderly into his kiss, but Matt didn't linger over it as much as he would have liked.

"It's late. I'll be back early in the morning, and then you have a long day ahead."

The soft sigh she let out made him smile. He wasn't alone in feeling reluctant to end this evening.

"Can you help me take these off before you go?" The earrings clipped on—they would have been far too heavy to thread through a hole in an earlobe—and the bracelet unclasped with ease. But Matt could see the mechanism holding it together at the back of her neck was complicated. And the tiara was held in place with tiny pins that dipped and tucked into the elaborate twist her stylist had pulled her hair back into.

Matt took his time locating each hairpin, pulling it out and laying it on the bathroom counter until at last the tiara was free. He loosened the pins that held the twist in place and removed each of them as well. He fluffed his hands through her hair, feeling the waves and curls that had set in from being wrapped in the formal style.

He lowered his hands and tinkered with the necklace, sliding his fingers under the heavy stones and lifting them up. He grazed her collarbone in passing and smiled to himself that if nothing else, he'd have sweet dreams tonight.

"What kind of stones are these? It's a stunning set, and they all seem to be perfectly matched."

"They are Petroberyl. It's the national stone of San Petro. They're not mined anywhere else in the world. This set belonged to my mother. I inherited it, so to speak, when she died. Technically, it belongs to the state, as part of our national jewels. But when I wear it, I feel closer to her. Carlos knows this is my favorite—that's why he brought it with him."

"They're gorgeous. Your mother would be proud."

Anneliese looked in the largest stone at the top of the tiara, holding it almost like a mirror. "I hope so. Things have been tough lately. Obviously, there was the broken engagement. Then my father's stroke. Then my brother taking over my father's duties and acting as though he cares for no one but himself. I often find myself wishing she was still here so I could just talk to her one more time. If I could ask her the questions on my heart, I know she'd have the answer. She always did."

Matt placed his palm on her heart. "I think if you listen, you'll still receive the answers you seek. Remember to speak up, Anneliese. Even if it's just to your own heart."

He dropped a kiss on the crown of her head and melted a little at how such a simple touch pulled him down like an undertow. He'd fallen so in love with this woman, but it wasn't his place to say so. He'd just have to hope his gestures brought her comfort and security and love. He'd just have to hope she knew.

"I'll see you in the morning, Annie. Be ready to live your dreams."

"Come on, slowpoke. You're going to miss the trolley."

A red streetcar came into view around the corner. It looked much like one Anneliese had ridden in San Francisco as a girl, but this one rolled on regular street tires instead of rails.

"Where are we going?" She caught up to Matt at the trolley stop after giving a most undignified version of a jog to make up the distance between them.

"Breakfast at the historic Guenther House. Built in the middle of the nineteenth century, the building is listed on the National Register of Historic Places. It was the home of the famous Pioneer Flour Mills family and today serves the best breakfast in San Antonio. There are those who say it's the best breakfast in America."

They took a seat in the middle of the blue line trolley, and Anneliese lost herself in watching the architecture of the city as they moved from the River Walk district to where the Guenther House was located, a few minutes away.

Once they reached the restaurant, they were seated under a massive pergola-style arbor outside the main house.

"Matt—this is charming! I love everything about it. Look at the beautiful white stone of the house."

"That would all be local. There's lots of gorgeous limestone in this part of the country. It's still a very popular building material for homes these days—either as a full stone façade or as accents mixed with brick or other materials."

"It's just beautiful. And the weather is gorgeous perfect too. Is Fall in Texas always like this?" Anneliese hadn't even had time to open her menu. She only had eyes for the picture-perfect surroundings.

And the man who had brought her here.

"Fall in Texas is like every other season in Texas. Unpredictable and ever-changing." He stopped himself and laughed. "Well, except for summer. That one is very predictable. It's always hot."

"We usually stay between seventy-five and eighty-five degrees Fahrenheit all year long. San Petro is very temperate."

"Maybe I'll come to escape the Texas heat one of these days."

He leaned back in his chair slightly and opened his menu. Anneliese couldn't see his eyes—they were hidden by aviator-style sunglasses—and she couldn't see the lower half of his face behind the cover of the menu.

"Are you serious about visiting San Petro? Or are you just saying that?" She really wanted to know the answer.

"Why wouldn't I be serious?" Matt continued to scan the menu as he talked. "It's your home, a place you love. Of course I'd like to see it."

Her heart tugged as it tried to leap, but practicality kept Anneliese from letting it take flight. If the press had a field day over her break up from Rafael, she couldn't begin to imagine what they'd say about her with Matt. They'd misunderstand the work that he did at Helping Hands Homes, write him off as a construction worker—and sneer that he was an American.

She wouldn't expose Matt to the mean-spirited, gossip-fueled paparazzi that followed her around simply because of the parents she was born to.

Anneliese picked up her menu and began to read through her options—it seemed far more pleasurable than dwelling on one of the worst aspects of her life, an aspect she would never willingly expose Matt to.

"I'd ask what's good here, but I imagine everything is."

"Exactly. But I'd recommend that you order the same thing I am going to—the breakfast platter. It comes with fluffy biscuits, fresh-made jam, and smoked bacon or sausage. I'll probably ask for a couple of eggs on the side. Breakfast perfection."

Anneliese laid her menu flat on the table. "Perfection. I like the sound of that."

As they ate, Matt told Anneliese about the history of the area. Although San Antonio was known for Mexican food and the Battle of the Alamo was between the Texans and the Mexican forces, there was also a strong German influence in the area, especially just north of San Antonio in the areas of Fredericksburg and New Braunfels.

"Port Provident played a major role in German immigration to Texas. It was the largest port in Texas at the time, and not far from the lighthouse was the center that processed tens of thousands of immigrants during the eighteenth century. The port was especially popular with German travelers, and many of them made their way right up to the heart of the Texas Hill Country," Matt shared.

Anneliese found that she enjoyed the history lesson almost as much as the fluffy biscuits and sticky jam thick with fruit. In fact, she realized, the history lesson edged out the biscuits for one reason alone —it allowed her to listen to Matt's voice for most of the morning.

As they waited for the trolley, Matt announced the next set of plans. "From here, we leave our German history and move back to a stronger Spanish influence. We're going shopping at *La Villita.*"

The Little Village. Judging by the name alone, Anneliese assumed this next destination would remind her of home. They boarded the next trolley back toward the River Walk. As they rode, Matt explained that La Villita was a little walled-in area at the edge of the River Walk.

"Many of the homes here date to the beginning of the eighteenth century, like as far back as 1811 and 1818, historians think. It was one of San Antonio's first neighborhoods. At the end of the 1930s, the mayor began restoring the area as part of the project to build the River Walk."

The surrounding walls were made of roughened white stone, and the criss-cross of streets was paved with cobblestones.

"It's like *Viejo Villagio* in Rosada. It's the old town square—the streets are cobblestones there. Horses still clip-clop on the stones for the tourists. It's still picturesque, even after all these years. Baskets of brightly-colored bougainvilleas line every windowsill, and colorful paper art is strung between the houses."

She smiled, enjoying another connection between her homeland and a small corner of Texas—just like Rosada had a sister city in Port Provident.

They walked through the picture-perfect neighborhood hand-in-hand, and Anneliese found herself basking in the *now* of the moment as much as the fall sunshine. If thoughts of the future came to mind, she pushed them away. For this weekend, she resolved to live right in the moment—every single last moment she had of being simply Annie de Cotriaro, just an average girl who'd lost her heart to Matt McGregor… but sadly couldn't let him know it was in his hands.

As they filtered through the small shops full of colorful arts and crafts, Anneliese felt time grow very still. She was grateful.

"Annie, look over here. This is perfect for you." Matt stood in front of a case of silver jewelry.

Anneliese left a display of pottery and joined him at the glass.

He pointed to a set of earrings, a necklace, and a bracelet. The silver had been polished and reflected the glare of the overhead fluorescent lighting. Each piece of the set bore a small, three-dimensional bird in flight. When worn, the dangle-style earrings would have appeared that the birds were suspended on their own from the ears. The necklace featured a larger bird, wings inlaid with a delicate turquoise and coral design.

"That's beautiful craftsmanship. I can't imagine the hours of work it would take to create a set like that."

Matt gestured at the salesperson behind the counter. "We'll take that set."

His words surprised her. "Oh, no, Matt, I couldn't."

"Maybe not," he smiled. "But I could."

"You've already done so much for me this morning. I can't accept a gift like that."

"Annie, you've done so much for me since you showed up in Port Provident. I want to do this. And I want you to have something to remember your time here. It reminds me of you. A beautiful creature about to take off to her destiny. This bird would speak up. This bird would be heard. I can't give you a set of Petroberyl, but I can give you this."

The woman behind the counter gave each piece a brief polish, then wrapped them individually in soft pouch-style bags of white cloth, each closed with a bright yellow drawstring. "Will there be anything else, sir?"

"We need that, too." Matt pointed at a simple ring, inlaid with the same turquoise and coral stones and threaded with delicate wisps of sterling silver. "Can we see if it fits?"

"Of course." She pulled out the tray and plucked the ring from the velvet-lined display, then handed it to Anneliese. "This is a small ring, but your fingers look delicate. It just might fit."

Anneliese could feel a slight tremble in her right hand as she held it out. She hoped no one around her would notice. The woman slid the ring over Anneliese's knuckle and gave it a press at the base of her finger.

"Perfect," she declared.

Anneliese turned it slowly with her left hand, admiring the craftsmanship all the way around the circle. She looked up at Matt. The corners of his mouth turned up slightly. She could tell he felt the same level of admiration for the piece as she did.

"We'll take this, too," he said.

Matt paid for the purchase and Anneliese browsed aimlessly while he finished. She couldn't focus on anything she saw on the racks in front of her. Her mind was filled only with images of coral and turquoise and silver birds in flight.

As a member of the San Petran royal family, Anneliese was used to being given gifts—often jewelry—by visiting royals, dignitaries, and others of importance who came to her country. But most of them had been to impress her, to make the giver look good.

Matt had given her this set of shining silver and colorful stone for the completely opposite reason—he'd wanted to make her look good.

She knew well the difference between the two types of motivation and it made her emotional to think about going back to a life where heartfelt generosity wasn't always found.

"Come on, Annie, there's still more to see." Matt put his arm around her waist, and she felt the strange contradiction of being the bird ready to soar in flight—yet still being totally grounded by the feel of his arm resting just above her hip bone.

She'd come to Texas to learn lessons that would help her ascend, to be the princess of her people she knew she'd been born to be.

But here, in this little Spanish-influenced neighborhood that reminded her of home, she felt as down to earth as she'd ever felt in her life. Unexpectedly, she'd put down roots in Texas.

She leaned into the shelter of Matt's arms and wondered if she really could ever go home again?

Matt knew he'd never be able to give Anneliese an engagement ring, but something in his heart felt right about the silver band with the ornamental stones. Those stones had been a part of nature for practically time eternal. And now they circled Anneliese's finger, transferring that sense of timelessness to her.

He couldn't give her a vow until death do us part—although he couldn't keep his heart or his mind from wandering there. It was all he'd thought about during the hours in the truck on the way to San Antonio. The circular train of thought had kept him up all night in his hotel bed, knowing she was on the other side of the wall, unreachable.

But he could give her today. He could give her the memories of seeing sights she'd only read about in books. And he could give her a small, silver symbol as a promise that he'd never forget the impact she'd made on his life in a whirlwind of time.

For lunch, he took her to eat at a Mexican restaurant located on the tip of the River Walk. They sat outside under a colorful patio umbrella and watched the ducks and river barges of tourists swim by. When lunch was over, they walked across a bridge of arched stone to the other side of the San Antonio River where they waited in line for a boat tour of their own.

Hand-in-hand, they explored everything San Antonio had to offer.

Matt had never felt so at peace with the world around him.

He'd never felt so much turmoil about what would happen once the sun set on this brief weekend.

"Are you ready for the Alamo?"

The grin on Anneliese's face was born of childhood joy, of the sense of wonder and exploration that came when something new sparked your attention for the first time ever.

"I can't wait. I can't believe I'm finally going to get to see it—real Texas history."

"Annie, Texas history is all around you. We just happen to be headed to be the most hallowed ground. There it is. Look across the street. *Missión San Antonio de Valero*—better known as the Alamo."

The iconic stone façade, with its gentle Spanish mission curve over the top of narrow window portals, was set back from the modern street corner which now wrapped around it. Tourists posed for pictures, looking for just the right angle to capture the rugged beauty of the historic building.

"You know…it's smaller than I thought it would be," Anneliese said as she studied the Alamo complex from their vantage point across the street.

Matt nodded. "You're certainly not the first person to say that. But remember, just because the Alamo is now larger than life, she started out as a simple Catholic mission on the Mexican frontier. She was here to serve settlers and educate the Native Americans who lived in this area about Christianity. She was built to honor God and to work hard. This is not the full, original mission. What you see in front of you was the chapel of the mission."

Anneliese shaded her eyes with her hand, and Matt caught the glint of a shard of sunlight as it winked off her new ring. "That makes perfect sense. We can go inside, right?"

"Yes," Matt said, holding her hand as they crossed the street. He reached up and removed the baseball cap he'd been wearing, folding it awkwardly and tucking it in his back pocket. "No hats allowed inside. The Alamo is a shrine to those days in 1836 when bravery received a new battle cry—*Remember the Alamo!*—and all these years later, we still do."

As they walked through the main building of the Alamo, peering into rooms where the great names of Texas history had fought and died, Anneliese turned to Matt and with a whisper said, "It's incredible—you can feel the significance as you walk through. It's so quiet in here, but it's almost as if something's speaking to me."

Matt laughed in as low a tone of voice as he could. "That's Davy Crockett. He's saying his famous line—'You may all go to Hell, and I will go to Texas'."

Now it was Anneliese's turn to try and stifle a laugh. "Now there's an example of speaking up and being bold. I should channel my inner Davy Crockett when I get home."

"You should channel your inner Davy Crockett and do as he did—stay in Texas."

The words popped out of Matt's mouth before he had a chance to filter them. His stomach turned and matched the slightly damp chill that filled the Alamo's limestone walls. He shouldn't have said it, even if it was the truth.

How could he take it back without being a liar?

Anneliese turned from looking in a small room, where one could imagine William Barrett Travis writing his pleas for help that would then be smuggled to the outside world.

Matt could use a plea for help of his own right now.

She stayed silent for a moment, then tugged on his hand and walked him back out of the mission.

"And what if I do, Matt?" She asked the question the moment they were back out on the front plaza in front of the Alamo.

In the distance, the sound of the Lone Star flag flapping against its flagpole matched the staccato of his heart.

"I don't know, Annie," he finally admitted. "But you're my '*a ha*' moment. You're the one person I don't want to be without. The first day I met you, I underestimated you. I dismissed you. Then one day, you started spitting broken fingernails on my floor, and I realized the person with limits was me, not the pretty girl from the palace. And I didn't want to be that guy anymore. I wanted to see the full potential in everyone, and I wanted to help bring it out of them. You make my heart full, Annie."

She twisted the ring around her right finger. Matt saw a tremble in her shoulder that matched the gentle shake of the leaves on the trees around them as the October breeze played.

"You're my '*a ha*' moment, too, Matt."

His heart leaped. Maybe they could work this out. He was used to building things, solving problems. They could build a solution.

"But Matt," she stumbled over her words as the color in her eyes deepened three shades. "If I'm not there, then who am I? How do I help my people if I'm not with them? For better or worse, God placed me in my family for a reason, and I have a duty."

"I don't want you to walk away from your duty," Matt said, reaching for her hand. "But I can't let you walk away from me, Annie, without a fight. I thought I could. I thought I could just buy you a bird on a chain so you could pull it out twenty years from now and remember me—and then I'd just keep my mouth shut and let you go home. But I can't, Annie. Forgive me, but I can't."

"I know," she said softly and squeezed his hand.

The bubble of sunshine that had surrounded them and kept the reality at bay from a halcyon runaway road trip that was supposed to make her dream come true... Matt knew when the bubble burst—he felt the break in his heart.

Carlos had left one more surprise for them—courtside seats to the evening's basketball game between the San Antonio Spurs and the Houston Rockets. The AT&T Center was charged with shouts, stomps, claps, and an effusive sense of fan energy.

Anneliese sat in the padded chair on the aisle and wished she felt the same sense of excitement. Instead, she felt like a foul had been called on her. Everything that Matt had said resonated in her heart. She wanted to say it all back to him—and more.

But Anneliese took over, and Annie took a back seat.

Anneliese put duty first, set up the mask over her thoughts, and measured her words carefully.

Anneliese couldn't tell Matt that Annie wanted to stay. Anneliese couldn't tell Matt that Annie had fallen in love with him.

The worst part was she could tell Matt knew she was holding something back. For all their conversations about speaking up, their last moments in San Antonio would be spent with him knowing she was living a lie.

"I'm going to run up to the concourse, Annie. Do you want a drink? Or maybe nachos or something?"

"They have nachos at a basketball game?" Melted cheese and a scoop of guacamole might just be what she needed to soothe her heart. There was a lot to be said for comfort eating.

Matt stood from his chair and scooted in front of her so he could get to the aisle. "Well, probably not the kind you're used to. Round, salty yellow corn tortilla chips and a side of what we call nacho cheese sauce. I'm not entirely sure what it is, exactly, but it's generally neon orange."

She shook her head. No, that would not be the kind of comfort food she was looking for at all. "How about just a soda?"

"I can do that. Be right back."

With Matt gone, she thought about how strange it was to be completely alone in a sea of people. *Better get used to it, Annie…once you leave here, once you go back to San Petro, that's how it's going to be. You'll leave Matt behind, and you'll be alone, even though you're surrounded by an entire nation of people you were born to serve.*

San Petro wasn't even that far away from Port Provident, relatively speaking. But it was far enough away that she couldn't think of a way to serve her people from Texas.

On the one hand, a basketball arena seemed like a funny place to pray, but on the other, it seemed as good a spot as any. She was out of ideas on her own. She was out of peace. She needed some of both, and she couldn't think of any other place to find them.

Her lips moved, but no sound escaped them.

I can't stay. But I can't go. God, how do I get to be in two places at once?

The T-shirt cannon popped rolled-up bundles of cotton into the stands over her head. Each whoosh of the cannon hit her ears and her mind—and something jarred loose.

Ambassador de Palma.

He had served the people of San Petro faithfully. And he'd done so from the United States.

But now he'd gone home. And she was here.

Oh, thank you, God. Thank you for putting these pieces in motion long before I even knew I'd need pieces of a plan. She raised two fingers to her lips, gave them a gentle kiss, and let the sentiment float to Heaven.

Anneliese dug in her purse and pulled out her phone. With adrenaline-fueled fingers, she fired off a text to Carlos. Then she laid the phone in her lap and waited.

Shortly, Matt returned to the seats, a souvenir cup of soda in each hand. He placed one in the cup holder closest to Anneliese and the other in his own. She could see the bubbles of the soda collecting at the top, bumping around the ice.

She felt exactly like that. Carbonated.

She tugged at Matt's sleeve. He turned his face toward her. It was blank. She couldn't wait to wipe away the hurt and the confusion.

"There's a way," she said simply.

Matt tilted his head. "For what?"

"For me to stay here."

Suddenly, Matt's eyes brightened like the industrial-sized spotlights that shone down on the court from the high ceiling of the AT&T Center. "How?"

"Since I've been here, Carlos has called me periodically with updates. One of those that he gave me a little while back was that our ambassador to the United States had resigned, effective immediately, due to some health issues with his wife and unborn twins. They needed to return to San Petro and focus on their family. And it just occurred to me—he'd served our country faithfully without being in the country. No replacement has been named. Well, until now. I just texted Carlos to put the wheels in motion and make it happen."

Matt sloshed cola on his khaki shorts and carelessly wiped it off. "Annie, do you think it could work? Really?"

Hope lit a fire in her. She could have run up and down the court a hundred times with the professional athletes in front of her. "Why not? I've grown up right in the heart of our government. I've been trained my whole life as an informal diplomat. I have a strong interest in strengthening our bonds across the board with the United States— unlike my brother, who just wants American tourist dollars and nothing more. In my heart, Matt, I know I could do this job and do it well."

"In my heart, Annie, I know you could too. I know we could. Together. Think of the lives we could both change—you for the people of San Petro and me with the continued work at Helping Hands. It could be incredible. Together, *we* could be incredible."

"Together, we *will* be incredible."

She looked up at the video board that hung over the court like a giant, futuristic LED chandelier. The screen was trimmed with a pink frame that declared the "Kiss Cam" was on. The camera panned through the crowd, then landed on Matt and Anneliese and zoomed in.

For once, Anneliese didn't mind being on TV. She was happy to oblige the "Kiss Cam" now—and forever.

8

―――――――

he knock at the hotel room door woke Matt up at first light.

He looked through the peephole in the door and saw Anneliese standing in the hallway. He opened the door without hesitation.

"What's wrong?" Matt knew something had happened. She was fully dressed in a trendy mocha-colored lightweight sweater and dark-wash skinny jeans that tucked into the tops of knee-high brown leather boots with a stacked heel.

She wasn't exactly dressed for sightseeing in San Antonio.

"Do you know a place called Austin Bergstrom International Airport?" she asked as she stood near the door he'd closed behind her with a soft click.

"I do. It's about an hour and a half from here—maybe a little less if we take the toll road. Why?"

"Carlos has a flight to San Petro booked for me. It leaves at ten-thirty this morning. I have to go home. Someone else will collect my things in Port Provident."

Matt ran his hand through his bedhead. "I don't understand."

"It's my father. He's had some unforeseen complications from the stroke. The word is they've moved up the vote on the succession laws so they can have it decided in case something happens to my father."

Her voice sounded as bleak as a winter sky.

"If the vote passes in my favor, I can't come back."

For all the hope Matt had felt when she'd told him about her plan last night at the game, he'd known in his battered heart it was too good to be true. There would always be something, some duty that would be waiting in front of Anneliese.

Whether it was standing vigil with her father or being handed the keys to rule the kingdom herself, her life and her duty were in San Petro.

Port Provident was just an island she came to visit for a time.

Matt was just an *"a ha!"* moment she'd had for a while.

What he needed to do now was *his* duty.

"I'll get you home to the people who need you most, Anneliese. Give me fifteen minutes to shower and pack and then we can go. It won't take long to get there."

"Matt?" She laid her hand on the lever that opened the door to the room. "You still need me, don't you?"

He wished he'd had the courage of William Barrett Travis, who'd penned a final defiant note at the Alamo, defiantly closing it with the words "victory or death" and assuring readers in a postscript that he felt God was on the side of the Texan fighters.

"I'll be okay. You go home. They need Princess Anneliese."

She slipped out of his room and back down the hall.

Matt leaned his head on the door as it closed behind her.

Victory or death, the Alamo commander had said in 1836. Matt didn't see either easing the pain he felt now. He wasn't going to win this fight—he couldn't compete with the family, the subjects, the duty she had before her in San Petro. And he wouldn't be granted oblivion from the pain, either.

He needed Anneliese in his life, but much like the defenders of the Alamo, he could see the reality in front of him.

He had to let her fly away.

Anneliese sat at the end of a long row of chairs in the waiting area that connected to the gate of her flight. On the concourse, she could see small restaurants serving barbeque and promising to "Keep Austin Weird." Colorful banners hung from the ceiling advertising the computers and other technology made by hometown employer Dell.

It was an airport, but everything buzzed with life and excitement.

Except her.

She sat in the open seat, looking out the window at the planes filing in. She'd put headphones in her ears, looking for some distraction while she waited.

If she thought about what was behind her, she'd get wrapped up in thoughts of Matt and all the things that were between them and all the things that could have been—if only she'd truly been Annie de Cotriaro instead of just pretending to be someone ordinary for a while.

If she thought about what was ahead, she became filled with fear over her father's health and unease about the idea of the vote ahead.

An airline employee tapped her on the shoulder, breaking up the mess that she couldn't keep her mind off of, no matter how hard she tried.

"Your Royal Highness, you'll be boarding first. If you'll come with me, I'll see to it that you're seated before we let anyone else on the plane. Again, I apologize that our VIP lounge is closed for repairs right now."

Back to being royalty. Back to a world where she smiled no matter if the sun was shining or the clouds were raining.

Anneliese pulled her mouth into a smile and stuffed her headphones and phone into her purse.

"It hasn't been an inconvenience at all. The staff has graciously taken care of me, and I appreciate all of your efforts."

She followed the woman in the dark navy uniform through a side door and then down the ramp to the plane. All of the crew working the flight had lined up in the doorway to greet her. Several tipped their heads in a quick, deferent bow. None of them were citizens of San

Petro, so none were expected to do so—but in Anneliese's experience, everyone wanted to do the right thing around royalty, so they tended to over-exaggerate their standard actions and practices.

"Can I get your carry-on bag for you, Your Royal Highness? I can put it in this overhead bin." A man whose nametag read "Jesse" gestured at the leather bag she'd brought with her.

"That's very thoughtful of you. Thank you."

As he lifted it up, Anneliese placed a hand on his arm and stopped him.

"One moment please—I need to get something out."

He placed the bag in the seat next to her. Anneliese unzipped it and fished her hand in, easily finding the white cloth bag with the yellow string tie that she'd placed on top.

"Thank you. This is all I needed." She held it in her hands and felt the shapes of birds in flight and a circle that fit her finger perfectly.

It all reminded her of Matt—everything she needed and everything she could never have.

"I don't want to see anyone when I get home, Carlos." Anneliese shuffled through some papers her private secretary had brought along with him in the limousine that picked her up from the airport. "Set some time aside for me to see Papa, and that's it."

"I'm sure when your brother finds out you've returned, he'll want to speak with you."

She cocked an eyebrow. "I'm sure he will. But he'll have to wait."

Anneliese scanned a briefing on where things stood as of yesterday with the succession vote. She thought to herself that she'd had to leave Annie back in Texas, but she'd made a concerted effort to bring Annie's spirit back home with her.

She didn't want to walk calmly in someone's shadow anymore.

She'd learned her worth in Texas, and she wanted to use it to do the most good she possibly could.

Back at *El Palacio de Rosada*, the palace the de Cotriaro family had called home for centuries, Anneliese entered through a back door and walked straight into her suite of rooms.

"Let me know when I can see Papa," she said to Carlos, then closed her door with a click and locked it behind her.

She wasn't about to take a chance that Federico would barge in and start in on whatever nonsense he felt he needed to say. She needed to see her father first. Papa was her priority. Everything else could fall in line later.

She had all the time in the world.

Her Royal Highness Princess Anneliese was home and wasn't leaving San Petro again.

About two hours later, Carlos knocked on the door. "Your father can see you now."

Her knees knocked a little bit. She hadn't been able to tell Papa she was leaving—he wouldn't have really understood, anyway. The stroke had tangled his thought processes like a plate full of spaghetti.

As she and Carlos walked the length of the palace to the far wing which had been set up like a hospital just for the king, Anneliese let her thoughts turn upward. With every footstep, she prayed that today would be one of Papa's good days.

She needed to talk to him. She needed his advice. She so wanted to be the confident, strong Annie she'd come to believe she could be, but in her heart, she knew a girl would always need her papa's advice and wise counsel. She'd missed those far-reaching, deep conversations since the stroke had peeled her father away from her, layer by layer.

Carlos knocked on the door to the wing, and the door opened silently on a hydraulic-style hinge. No expense had been spared to make this small unit as complete and comfortable as a hospital and rehabilitation facility. Whatever treatment the king needed, he would find it behind this heavy door.

"Welcome home, Your Royal Highness." The king's personal physician, Dr. Enrique de León, greeted her first. "He's glad to have a visitor."

"Is today a good day?" Anneliese extended her words with caution.

"He seems to be more alert this afternoon. He had a rough morning, but I'm pleased with how he is doing right now. I can update you more once you come out."

"That sounds good, thank you."

Tentatively, Anneliese opened the door to the solitary patient room in the specialized hospital unit.

"Papa?"

He shifted his hand slightly, but the wave was small. Had she not seen the tubing of the IV move, she might have missed his subtle greeting.

Anneliese sat down in the padded visitor's chair next to him and took his thin hand. He was a shell of the man he'd once been, but it still felt comforting to have him beside her.

"Good trip?" His words slurred, but she loved that he remembered she'd been gone and could ask about it.

"Yes. Port Provident is a great place full of wonderful people. It is a true sister city for Rosada."

"That is good." One corner of his mouth twitched in an approximation of a smile. It broke Anneliese's heart to see the other side of his once-strong face lying motionless.

So much to talk about filled her mind. She knew there was no way she'd be able to have the long, thoughtful conversation she longed for. She needed to pull together what her most important thoughts were and what she thought her father would be most likely to be able to respond to.

"I learned a lot. I met a lot of local leaders, I helped raise funds, I saw a community center with a temporary medical clinic and processing center for donations. I helped renovate a house. I feel like I have gained so much that we will be able to use the next time a disaster like a hurricane strikes San Petro. I hope it won't be for a long, long time—but whenever it may come, I know I have the knowledge I need to bring together charities and government to best help our people."

"Good, good." The accompanying squeeze of her father's hand felt like the flutter of a hummingbird's wings—paper light and gone in a split second. "You saw Foster and George?"

"I did, Papa. They came out to see the Helping Hands Homes project I worked on and then held a fundraising dinner and named me the guest of honor."

"You liked it?"

Anneliese felt the stirring of a voice whispering in her ear. *Speak up. Be bold.*

"Papa, can I ask you something? I know you may not be able to answer, just do the best you can."

His head approximated a nod, and he made a positive grunt of affirmation. She took it as the green light to move forward.

"Have they told you there's a vote pending in Parliament to change the rules of succession to reflect the oldest child, not just the oldest male?"

The king closed his eyes and breathed out with more force than she'd seen since she entered the room. "Your brother…no."

There were so many ways she could have interpreted that. She didn't want to pressure her father or make him expend any more energy than necessary, but she needed to know what he meant.

"No what, Papa? He doesn't support it?"

There was a long pause before the answer came. Anneliese felt the mask that concealed her father's true thoughts dropping. She'd been raised with one too and had only dropped hers for one person—Matt.

She knew he was struggling to get the words just right.

"No. He does not. But he should not rule." He took a deep breath, relying heavily on the supplementary oxygen that made it easier for him to get enough air in his lungs. "Cannot influence decision though. So how can I help you?"

The last words came out in a measured beat like a drum, one syllable at a time.

They were unmistakable.

She wanted to be respectful of the gift her father had just bestowed on her. She'd waited her whole life to hear that she was good enough to represent her people, to rule San Petro. But she also understood her father couldn't be seen as meddling in the affairs of the democratically-elected Parliament. The monarch of San Petro had a unique partnership with Parliament, different from every other monarchy remaining in the world.

"I don't know, Papa. I would like to see how the process plays out. I guess we will know soon, right?"

He left his eyes closed as he leaned back on the pillow. "Soon."

She kissed him gently on the forehead. His skin felt dry and thin. "I'll let you get some rest, but I'll be back, and we can talk more."

He pressed his lips together, returning the kiss as best he could. "Good."

"I love you, Papa."

"Love. You."

"We need to talk." Federico grabbed Anneliese by the arm as she walked back through the palace.

"It's good to see you too, *hermano*." She tried to address her brother as formally and respectfully as possible, but it quickly became apparent that the fuse of his temper had already been lit, regardless of anything she was going to say or do right now.

He didn't release his grip on her arm, and instead jerked her into the palace's formal library on their left.

"Did you think you could just pack up and leave without telling me? I'm running this kingdom now. You have to get my permission for anything you do."

In her mind's eye, she saw a lighthouse, an island, and a brown-haired man with work boots who had given her the freedom to be exactly who she wanted to be. Her heart ached for the autonomy. Her heart ached for the respect. Her brother didn't know how to give either.

"Maybe not for long. There will be a vote. Parliament will decide who officially succeeds Papa."

She spoke with low and deliberate tones. Getting into a forceful yelling match with her brother was not her style—but she did want to ensure he knew that she knew his days of bullying and power might well be numbered.

Federico threw his head back and laughed. Immediately, Anneliese's nerves leaped to the edge. She could feel the sharpness of the razor's blade they now sat on. Why would he laugh about something so serious?

"Not anymore."

Surely he was wrong. She'd just come from speaking about it with Papa. He would be given the most updated and accurate information. After all, regardless of lying in a hospital bed, he *was* still the king.

"You're wrong." She tried calling her brother's bluff.

"No. I'm not." He pulled a piece of paper from his pocket and pushed it close to her face. Anneliese scanned the few lines of text quickly. "I got that stopped. There's no reason to go changing laws that have served us well for centuries."

A light went off in Anneliese's head, brighter than all the glow generated by the massive video boards in the AT&T Center only a matter of hours before.

She'd heard those words before. Carlos had briefed her on Speaker Carretierez's thoughts.

And those had been the Speaker's thoughts—word for word. Now Anneliese knew where those thoughts had come from—the one man with the most to lose.

His Royal Highness Crown Prince Federico of San Petro.

"I don't know what stunt you were trying to pull, Anneliese, but you're not going to get away with it. I'm in charge here, and it's going to stay that way."

Speak up.

The voice in her head challenged her, pushed her to take the exact action she needed to. Without that time in Port Provident, without those lessons she learned, she wouldn't have stepped up to this battle with her brother. She wouldn't have pulled out the sword of truth to defend her fellow San Petrans.

"Where's your vision for the people, Federico? You want to turn this island into some kind of Caribbean Monte Carlo, full of fast cars and fast money." Instinctively, her hands moved defiantly to her hips. "That may be all well and good for you, but how does that help the people of San Petro? What about their hopes and dreams? What about your responsibility to them?"

"My responsibilities aren't really your concern, Anneliese. They're not your responsibilities. In fact, you don't really have responsibilities here—just go keep visiting your charities and cutting ribbons. Then you can get married—well, if you can keep a man around—and go cut ribbons wherever he lives."

Anneliese couldn't remember a time when she and her brother could call themselves friends, but his cruel statement overstepped every boundary that had ever existed around them.

She'd never heard him speak to her with such contempt.

Her pulse began to race. She felt her jaw stiffen and her shoulders lay back.

If she stayed here, her brother would continue to marginalize her. Clearly, they didn't see eye-to-eye, and he saw her as a problem, not part of the solution.

A thought slowly began to rise in her head, like the sun slipping above the water at the break of morning and floating higher and higher until it reached a peak.

She could end this conversation today without ending it permanently.

She could still put the plan to serve as San Petran ambassador into motion. One word from Papa would take care of that. It would give her access to the halls of Parliament and those who would support her for her plans for the future as the monarch of San Petro. It would give her valuable experience in statesmanship to go along with her "ribbon cutting skills."

It would give her the opportunity to speak up.

And when the time was right, with careful planning and preparation, she believed the vote could happen—and go in her favor.

Anneliese could no longer sit idly by and let things happen to her and be said about her without standing up and speaking up. She needed to be that woman that Pastor Ruiz described, both for herself and for the men, women, and children of her country. And to do that, she'd need the courage and spirit she'd felt at the Alamo as she'd walked through the building where bravery and boldness had taken a stand.

"Federico?" Anneliese spoke through a clenched jaw.

"What?"

The time was now. *Speak up, Anneliese!* She willed boldness through her body, envisioning the fighting spirit riding through her veins with her blood.

"You may go to Monte Carlo, and I will go to Texas."

Matt swung his hammer and forced his mind to remember that nothing had really changed.

Unfortunately for him, the only thing his mind wanted to remember were take-out dinners by the red-and-white striped lighthouse, a tiara sparkling in the light of a ballroom, and walking hand-in-hand in the shadows of Texas' greatest legends.

All he wanted to remember was Anneliese.

He pounded another nail into a sheet of drywall. He pushed aside thoughts of another house, another sheet of drywall, and another assistant who held the thick white rectangles as he fixed them in place.

The truth was simple. She'd already been gone a few more days. In a few weeks, she'd be gone longer than she ever had been around.

Anneliese de Cotriaro was a firefly. She floated into his life when he least expected it, twinkled for a moment, and then was gone. You couldn't hold creatures like that, nor could you trust them. It was better that he learned that hard lesson now, after a few weeks, instead of later. Anneliese's duty would always be to San Petro.

He'd seen it up close in their time together. Her first duty wasn't even to herself. It was to her people and to the responsibilities she shouldered on their behalf.

If her first thoughts were never even of herself, Matt knew they'd never be of him. It would always be like that. He definitely couldn't begrudge Anneliese her reality. But he could take a step back, take another swing with the hammer, and be silently thankful that it had not become his reality.

"Hey, Matt!" Dave called across the room.

Matt lost the limited focus he had and brought the hammer straight down on his thumb. He muttered something under his breath and was thankful his boss couldn't hear exactly what he'd just said.

He was also thankful for something that hurt worse than the memories of Anneliese. It didn't make much sense to appreciate a busted thumb, but he'd take any distraction he could get right now.

Matt raised his thumb in a cocky salute. "Hey there, Dave. What's going on?"

"I need to talk to you about a couple of things—do you have a minute?"

"It's probably going to be a good five minutes until I get the feeling back in my thumb, so you can have those." He turned his hand over and looked at the thumb from all angles. That was going to leave a mark.

"Great. Let's go outside. It's a little loud in here—but that's a good thing. We're moving along nicely, aren't we?"

"We are." Matt looked around the room, and as he did, the smells of a house-in-progress filled his nose. He actually liked the various tangy scents because they reminded him work was going on and every day was one day closer to having another family back home on the island in a safe place to live.

"So I've been approached by a donor with a bold idea," Dave said as they both sat down on a large ice chest in the front yard. "They'd like to help us take Helping Hands Homes internationally, and I'd like you to help lead that effort."

Matt considered both halves of Dave's statement carefully. "I think that's a great idea. There's so much work we can do around the world. But Dave, I have a job here—at least until December."

"This is effective January first. You're our new International Director."

He'd be finished with the Port Provident project by then. Maybe it was time to do something different. "What's involved?"

He decided to keep his cards pretty close to the vest, in case David said something that didn't interest him.

"More travel. Going to these countries and checking out the infrastructure, making partnerships with their governments and NGO resources already in the area. Setting up what we need on the ground to have a local and long-lasting presence in the area, as well as being able to respond quickly when there are disasters. Your experience here in Port Provident is just what the donor and I are looking for in order to get this off the ground."

Matt couldn't deny the idea was intriguing. He'd be getting his hands dirty in a whole new way, broadening the reach of the work Helping Hands was doing into communities that genuinely needed a helping hand.

"I'd like to see you also connect with that doctor over at that church thing that's been in the news. My vision goes beyond just homes. I want to be on the ground creating one-stop points of contact for home renovation, medical care, and more. I want us to be a factor for good around the world in as many areas as we can."

"You mean Dr. Pete Shipley at The Grace Space?" Matt remembered getting the tour of the facility with Anneliese and how excited she had been at what a handful of volunteers and some determination, paired with a vision, had been able to accomplish.

"I guess so. It's the church with the Spanish name."

"*La Iglesia de la Luz del Mundo.* Yeah, I can work with them. That's a really interesting idea."

Dave slapped his palms on the knees of his jeans. "So you're in?'

Matt thought about priorities. He thought about the chance to work with people around the world and really make a difference in their lives. He'd always been interested in that—he wouldn't have been a part of Helping Hands Homes for so many years if he hadn't. His great-aunt Diana Peoples had sparked the family tradition of service in him way back in his childhood.

And then he'd seen a princess travel to another country, driven by a desire to grow and learn and help.

If he'd had to say goodbye to Anneliese sooner than he'd have liked, at least he now knew how he could honor those lessons he'd learned.

He wasn't going to have her in his life ever again, but the interests and goals they shared in common…well, he could still keep those.

His thumb had stopped throbbing. His mind had stopped spinning. For the first time since Anneliese knocked on his hotel door in San Antonio, the world made sense again.

Matt was going to move on with his life. No regrets. No looking back.

After the volunteers on the latest Helping Hands Homes project went back to their regularly-scheduled lives in Houston for the evening, Matt locked the door to the house behind him and began to drive back to the hotel. As he passed the 15th Street intersection, he abruptly U-turned, as though his truck had found the auto-pilot gear.

The next phase of his life had started today. There was no sense in putting off conversations and details. He wanted to talk to Pete Shipley over at The Grace Space.

Besides, the only other alternative he had this evening was to sit at the lighthouse alone with only a Styrofoam take-out container for company.

Matt's footsteps echoed on the concrete floor inside of The Grace Space. There were only two or three people inside the building. Everyone else had moved outside for the evening, to gather for the home-cooked meal prepared by the ladies of the church.

He tried not to think of the mouth-watering lunch he'd shared here or the heart-stopping woman he'd shared it with. Everything about this afternoon had been Matt willing his mind to move on. Why could he not stop thinking about someone he'd known for such a relatively short time?

It made no sense.

"*Señor* McGregor! Welcome back! How may I help you?" Pastor Marco Ruiz walked down an aisle of donated bedding and other linens as he made a bee-line for Matt.

"Hi, Pastor Ruiz," Matt said, admiring the neat stacks of donated items available for the citizens of Port Provident to take what they needed most. "I was looking for Dr. Shipley."

"Oh, he had to run an errand with Angela's daughter, Celina. Is there something I can help you with?"

"I'm not sure. I was just approached today by my boss that a donor has come forward and wants to make Helping Hands Homes international. One of the things he wants to introduce into our blueprint in the countries where we're going to work is something like what's being done here at The Grace Space."

The pastor's eyes lit up like a traffic light turning to green. "That would be wonderful. Dr. Shipley is definitely who you want to talk to. I know he's had conversations about making this a permanent structure in Port Provident. It's wonderful to see all the interest in what's going on here."

"Can you let him know I stopped by?" Matt pulled a business card out of his wallet and handed it to Pastor Ruiz. "This has my cell phone on it. He can call me at any time, and we can schedule some time to talk when it's convenient for him."

The pastor took the card and tucked it in his own wallet. "Now, would some dinner be convenient for you?"

He walked over to Matt and put an arm around his shoulder, then gestured toward the crowd outside with his other hand.

Matt had driven by this church thousands of times during his time growing up in Port Provident. But he'd never once stopped. Never once thought about the people who gathered and worshipped here. And something inside ached at that realization.

How long had he stayed on his side of town and missed out on getting to know people who loved this town as much as he did?

He couldn't deny that both times he'd been here, he'd found optimism and generosity, freely given in spite of the devastation and tragedy all around.

And because of that, Matt's first instinct was to shake his head. He didn't have optimism to give in return tonight, no matter how hard he tried to "No, Pastor, I really can't."

"Can't?" He smiled with a knowing grin. "Or won't?"

Matt laughed, caught in the trap of semantics. "Maybe it's a little bit of both. I do have some work I need to take care of tonight. Payroll and things like that."

"Well, you can't do payroll on an empty stomach. And the ladies of the church have been making tamales. This has been an enormous undertaking. They partnered with a church on the mainland to do most of the cooking this afternoon. Trust me, you won't want to miss this."

As they walked out the door, Matt could smell the familiar scents of pork and masa. He'd always loved Mexican food. Of course, now, it made him think of the tamale perched on the left edge of the combination plate he'd ordered at the Mexican restaurant beside the San Antonio River. He remembered brightly colored outdoor umbrellas and the bright smile of the woman across the table from him.

A frustrated breath escaped his nostrils before he had a chance to stop it, and the forceful push of air made a low growling sound in his throat.

"Something's troubling you, *Señor* McGregor."

"You can call me Matt, Pastor. I've seen your church sanctuary without carpet. We don't have to be this formal." He tried to make a joke, tried to laugh it all off.

But the pastor wasn't fooled. "And you can call me Marco. But I can tell something's wrong. I'd like to help if I can. You're not a member of my congregation, but I think you'll find I have pretty good listening ears."

Marco paused and then directed them toward a set of chairs underneath a wind-battered palm tree. "How's the Princess? I don't see her with you today."

Matt's head craned. He gave the pastor a level look. "She's back home in San Petro."

"Well, that explains it." Marco acted as if that one statement answered it all.

"Explains what?'

"You're preoccupied, my friend. You came to talk to Pete about the operations at The Grace Space, but if he had been here, you wouldn't have heard a word he said, now would you?"

"No, probably not," Matt admitted morosely. "You've got me there."

"So why did she go home?"

"Duty called." Matt shrugged. It was the most accurate and straightforward explanation he knew.

"And why did you not go with her?" Marco continued to probe.

"My duty is here. I have homes to rebuild." Matt gazed blankly at the parking lot, trying not to focus on anything—especially his feelings about the situation. "This is my world. She has her own world. And I don't belong in it."

"Mateo," the pastor said, seamlessly changing Matt's name to the Spanish version, "you belong wherever God sends you. And sometimes you don't know where that is until you ask."

"Until I ask? Ask whom?"

"Well, I'm a pastor. Of course, I think you should ask God. I'm a big believer in the power of prayer. He does more than we could ask or imagine. I asked for help organizing donation trucks, and God brought me Pete Shipley, and now we have a store and a medical clinic together for the community." Marco pointed back at the building that housed a full-scale, multifaceted operation. "But in this case, I think you should ask her too."

He made another grunting noise. *McGregor, get yourself together*, he scolded in his mind.

"Well, I can't just call the palace. I don't think they're listed in the phone book." He took a deep breath and tried to calm himself down. It wasn't fair to take out his frustrations on Marco. "Look, man, I know you're trying to help—and I appreciate it, I really do. But I don't want to call her. I'd just rather forget her. She made it clear that her duty will always come first. I just need to respect that."

One of the church ladies walked toward them, carrying a loaded plate in each hand. Now Matt made more unplanned noises as his stomach let out a large grumble. So much for being able to deny he wanted dinner so he could get out of here sooner.

"Gracias, Juanita." Marco reached for the first plate. "Matt, do you know Juanita Garcia? She owns Huarache's Restaurant on Gulfview Boulevard."

Matt reached up and took the other proffered plate. "We've never met, but I do know her restaurant. It's been one of my favorites here in town for years. I'm Matt McGregor. It's nice to meet you."

"It's nice to meet you too. You both looked like you could use some home cooking." She smiled with a warmth equaled only by the hot steam coming off the plate, then eyed Matt with the pointed gaze of a mother. "You look like you need to speak up about something. You're among friends here. You don't have to bite your tongue."

Speak up.

That was the phrase Anneliese had latched on to—more specifically, that was the phrase Annie had adopted as her own statement of vision and empowerment. It had changed her life.

Too bad it couldn't change his.

What was done, was done.

Matt began to stab at the tamale in front of him with his fork. He was as done with this conversation as he was with memories of Annie.

Too bad Pastor Ruiz wasn't. "You know, Matt, I talked with your Princess Anneliese about speaking boldly. We were talking about speaking on behalf of her people, but you know there are other means of speaking up."

Matt decided to keep himself from speaking at all. He stuffed a bite of tamale in his mouth and began to chew slowly. He appreciated the clean flavor of the masa alongside the spiciness of the pork like he'd appreciated nothing since the long, quiet drive back to Port Provident after dropping Anneliese off at the airport in Austin.

There was her name again. Why wouldn't it just go away?

Pastor Ruiz picked up on the extended beat of silence between them and decided to fill it. "Anyway, I would just remind you, my brother, that there's the power of life and death in our tongues and the words we speak—or don't speak, as the case may be. The Bible says so. You're probably right, there's probably not a way to Google the phone line at the palace. But I know you're a smart guy, and you have a vision. You wouldn't have dreamed up this one hundred houses project if you weren't. And it's coming to fruition. That tells me you're a guy who makes things happen. And I think you'll know what you need to do when the time comes."

Matt looked at the space on his plate where the first tamale had once been. He felt crazy for even thinking philosophical thoughts about a tamale, but right now, it totally made sense to him.

"Pastor?" Matt directed his dinner companion's focus to the disposable plate. "This is how I feel right now. Something's missing. But I can't bring that tamale back, and I can't bring her back. I can just enjoy the time I had with each for what it was."

Marco nodded deliberately, then turned his gaze to the wisps of cloud that covered the orange-streaked sky like gauze.

"I understand, my friend. Just promise me that you'll remember one thing."

Matt didn't want any more memories messing with his head, but Marco's voice was as low and serious as it could possibly be. Matt knew he couldn't say no, couldn't make a joke, couldn't bluff his way out of this one.

"I promise."

"Just remember that sometimes the words we say—or the words we don't say—are a matter of life and death." The pastor gave Matt a clap on the shoulder. "When the time comes, I know you'll know what to do. Don't be afraid to speak up, my friend."

He rose and took his empty plate to the trash, leaving Matt alone to watch the sheer cotton cross the sky and wonder if the clouds looked the same from a small island in the Caribbean.

Within two weeks, Matt had settled into a dual role, spending his mornings on the job sites in Port Provident—thanks to the presidential fund money, they were able to have several homes in progress at the same time. With that turn of events, Matt spent a fair amount of time in his truck now. He drove to each house. A few days a week, he drove to a short meeting with Pete Shipley to brainstorm ideas for how to integrate The Grace Space concept into the Helping Hands Homes International model. The doctor had his own commitments and served only in an advisory capacity to Matt, but he seemed to very much enjoy the discussion about how to make the model sustainable.

And then, every afternoon, Matt drove to Houston for meetings about the international expansion. There were meetings with donors, meetings with suppliers, meetings with people who just seemingly loved to have meetings. And because a number of foreign countries had consular branches in the fourth-largest city in America, Matt found himself making a number of connections with diplomatic staff attached to countries which were interested in having a Helping Hands Homes presence.

He was encouraged by how well the concept was being received and how the details were coming together. He was encouraged by all the progress taking place on Port Provident in such a short time since Hope blew through.

And most of all, he was encouraged that staying very, very busy had kept his mind off the one train of thought he had no interest in riding.

This afternoon, though, Matt wasn't driving. He was waiting. A ceremony would be held today to turn over another set of keys to a Port Provident homeowner. The main office of Helping Hands Homes had arranged for a number of their international contacts to be on the island to take part so they could see for themselves the results of a Helping Hands Homes project.

Matt would be meeting the fifteen or so invited guests through a home in progress, then taking them to tour The Grace Space and talk with Pete Shipley for half an hour. Then they'd come back to the Turner family's house, turn over the keys, and welcome another family back to safe housing on Port Provident.

He stood on the side of the Barnes house, the house that was currently under construction. The group would be touring it first, and Matt wanted to go over an inspection report before the crowd arrived.

He leaned against the siding of the house, thankful that they'd been able to focus strictly on the interior of this property. The exterior had held up very well against the wind and water.

Matt heard the crunch of footsteps on grass but didn't look up. He wanted to make sure he understood everything in the report before the crowd got here—he didn't want to get distracted by someone on the work crew with so little time to himself before the day's activities began.

"Matt?"

Never had that one syllable shot so arrow-straight for his heart.

He lost all concentration in an instant and looked up from the now-uninteresting piece of paper.

All the hours, minutes, seconds he'd spent trying to keep this face out of his mind…and now it loomed a scant two feet from his eyes and the mind that had fought so valiantly to keep thoughts of her at bay.

"Anneliese?"

She played with the strap of her oversized black leather purse. "The Honorable Anneliese de Cotriaro, Ambassador to the United States for the Kingdom of San Petro. But you may call me Annie."

Matt gave her a square stare. "But what are you doing here? What about the vote? Why are you in Port Provident?"

"The vote…well, let's say it's been postponed. My father agreed that I had enough qualifications to be nominated to the post of ambassador and that it would give me a thorough education in diplomacy that would benefit the citizens of San Petro."

"So there was no vote?" Matt could barely focus on what Anneliese was saying. Mostly, he heard a low drone, like a hive of bees had invaded his ears.

It should have been a good sign. Seeing Anneliese again should have been a moment that was sweet like honey.

Instead of meeting those expectations, Matt found that he couldn't even think of her as Annie. In fact, he couldn't even think.

"But why are you here? This isn't Washington, D.C."

"I was invited. You didn't know the main Helping Hands office had invited me here today?"

Matt shook his head. "No, I hadn't seen a full list for today. At my briefing yesterday, they still had several spots unconfirmed."

"David called my office at the beginning of the week. He is interested in rolling out the international program first in San Petro."

Matt's mind spun around violently, as if it had been a car broadsided in an intersection. "I don't understand. This is my project. He should have told me."

"So you're mad that I'm here?" Her tone of voice shifted abruptly.

He couldn't say yes, and he couldn't say no. And then he remembered a bite of spicy tamale and thin clouds pulled across an orange sky. Matt remembered a conversation with Pastor Ruiz that he hadn't wanted to take part in—much like this current conversation with Anneliese.

The pastor had taken great care to emphasize that the words that *didn't* get said often had as much meaning as the words that were let free out of our mouths. And as much as he'd like to shut down and shut up, Matt realized that he couldn't do either.

"No. But I never expected to see you again. Not here, not anywhere. You made it clear that you had to leave immediately because of your duty to your country called. Now you're back, but you're here again out of duty with your country." Matt slowly lifted his head upward, squinting against the sun, weighing the power of life and death in his words. "I never expected to, Anneliese, but I told you that you were my '*a ha*' moment. I fell in love with you along the way. A guy who builds homes on the Texas coast could never deserve a Caribbean kingdom princess, so I kept quiet as best I could. But someone told me that there's just as much power in the words we say as the words we don't. So I can't keep quiet if we're working together going forward. I know you're back in the United States for duty, Anneliese. But is there a place for me anywhere? Or just the people of San Petro? I guess I just need to know before I can be a part of expanding Helping Hands to San Petro."

She started to answer, then Matt jumped back in the conversation. "No, that's not exactly right. I need to know before I walk over there and hand this family the keys to their house. I need to know before I take one more step, Anneliese."

As though on cue, she took one step forward, closing the gap between them to mere inches. Matt's pulse raised with a powerful cocktail of adrenaline, anticipation, and the smell of her perfume. Life and death, indeed. He could feel his heart pounding at an alarming rhythm that made him keenly aware that the hospital on the island was closed.

"I've told you before. Call me Annie." Her tone of voice gave no quarter. Her two simple sentences were not a request. They were a royal command.

"Annie," he replied, swallowing hard against the concrete that had formed at the top of his throat.

"I have a duty not just to my people, Matt," she said. "I have a duty to myself. I have a duty to speak up. My time here taught me that. I spoke up for this position, not just because I believe I can make a difference, but because I wanted to be back here for myself. I spoke up that I wanted to be based out of our Consulate in Houston for a time, not because it's conventional, but because it was important to me. And there's one more thing I need to speak up on as well."

"What's that?"

She was so close that Matt could feel a charge of electricity between them.

"I need to speak up and let you know that I love you too. You've got a new job that will take you all over the world. I've got a new job that will do much of the same. You said a guy who builds houses has no business being with a princess, but you're wrong. The bottom line is that we both care about people and we want to serve them. We're the same, Matt, regardless of our backgrounds."

The blood in his veins surged, then drained as he realized the weight of her words. But was a guy who knew about building, and above all, he knew that he could build more conflict in her life.

"I'm the guy that will make the tabloid press question your motives and your sanity. You don't need any more of that in your life. I don't have a crown to give you—or anything like that."

Anneliese placed a light finger on his lips, stilling the thoughts and fears and doubts that he couldn't hold back from speaking. She leaned her head a little closer, tilting it slightly.

"I have enough tiaras and jewelry to last me a lifetime. You have two things I don't have back at the *El Palacio de Rosada*."

He whispered gruffly. "What are those?"

"Your heart. And in time, your last name." She moved a fraction closer. "That is, if you're interested in sharing them with me."

Matt let the inspection report float to the ground as he reached his arms around Anneliese's shoulders and pulled her tightly to him, closing the tiniest of gaps that had remained between them.

"They're yours, Annie."

They'd both spoken up, but as Matt leaned down and met Anneliese's lips with his own, he knew that sometimes…words weren't even necessary.

EPILOGUE

Anneliese couldn't believe a year had passed since the morning she read the newspaper story about Hurricane Hope hitting San Petro. She'd chosen this day for her wedding to Matt specifically because it celebrated new beginnings.

Hurricane Hope had meant a new beginning for Port Provident.

It had meant the trip of a lifetime for Anneliese, where she found her voice, her mission, and her heart.

It had meant a dream fulfilled for Matt, as he rebuilt his hometown and saw his vision for helping others come to life around the world.

And it had been the start of a new beginning for the Kingdom of San Petro. Three months ago, Parliament had voted on streamlining the laws of succession to name the monarch's oldest child, regardless of gender, as the heir to the throne. She'd resigned her position as ambassador and settled back into daily life in San Petro, now as the Crown Princess.

None of the changes sat well with Federico, but after a high-speed car accident in the mountains of San Petro and several well-documented late-night parties, Parliament could no longer be persuaded that the old ways were still the best ways.

"Your Royal Highness?" Carlos Pampalón walked into the salon where dressers and attendants were putting the finishing touches on Anneliese's hair and makeup. "Mr. McGregor asked me to bring this to you."

He gingerly held out a large brown envelope. Anneliese took it and unwound the thread holding the flap down. She pulled out two pieces of paper, one a heavy white cardstock, and the other a faded thin paper that had been folded in thirds.

Dearest Annie,

There are only three known copies of this letter in the world—and even then, it is not as rare as what we've found together. When I heard this was being auctioned, I moved Heaven and Earth to present it to you on our wedding day. Whether this ends up in a museum or just in your private collection, I will always think of it as a testament to the weekend I fell in love with you and the fighting spirit embodied by both you and the man who wrote it.

I love you, and I will never be afraid to speak up and tell you so,

Matt

Gingerly, Anneliese unfolded the other piece of paper, careful to not let any tears of emotion at the words of the man who was about to be her husband slip onto the historic document.

The paper felt as thin and soft as rose petals between her fingers. The ink on the pages had faded, but the signature under the words "Victory or Death" was clear.

This was a letter from William Barrett Travis, commander of the

Alamo, pleading for reinforcements during those fateful March days in 1836.

Matt had once told her he had no crown to give her, but no diamonds could have meant more than this incredibly personal and historic gift. Carefully, she slid it back in the thick envelope and held it out to Carlos.

"Can you see that is taken to the San Petran archives immediately? I don't know what we will do with it—it seems like the right thing may be to send it home to Texas, I don't know. But I do want to make sure it is given the utmost care."

Carlos nodded. "Of course, Your Royal Highness."

Everyone had become so formal since her ascent to Crown Princess. Her father's health continued to improve, but there were still many day-to-day functions that she filled in his stead. Federico had decamped to Monte Carlo after the vote to lick his wounds, so it was just Anneliese and her father behind the palace walls now.

But Matt would be joining them soon, and he would be bringing his passion for helping others with him. Anneliese knew they would do great things in San Petro together.

She took one more look at the thoughtful words of love Matt had put down on the small note. Of all the documents she reviewed on a daily basis, this would be the most important she'd ever read.

The dress on the hook behind her, all satin and lace, was as crisp and white as the notecard Matt had inscribed his love upon. She looked from one symbol of love to the other and smiled, anxious to put on her gown and be not just the crown princess, but Matt McGregor's bride.

"Maria, I think it's time."

The cathedral in San Petro was a world away from the church he'd grown up in back in Port Provident. Matt forced himself to take a few deep breaths as he stood at the front of the grand building, listening to the strains of violin music.

The crowd outside had erupted into cheers only moments before, so Matt knew Anneliese had arrived.

He smiled, thinking that for once, the paparazzi would be taking photos and this time, they'd have only nice things to say about his beautiful bride.

Of course, her beauty wasn't just about her blonde hair, charming smile, and petitely-proportioned body. Her beauty came from her heart.

It was a heart of compassion, lived boldly, and he could not believe that as of today, he would be joined with that heart in the eyes of God —and everyone in the world who read the tabloids.

The musicians in the chamber changed their song, and the familiar strains of *Jesu, Joy of Man's Desiring* filled the cathedral to the rafters. Guests began to stand.

The heavily-carved wooden doors opened, and silhouetted against the stunning Caribbean sun was Anneliese. Her hair had been swept into an updo, and a tiara of diamonds and San Petran Petroberyl had been tucked in the waves. The bodice of the dress had been entirely covered in a tiny pattern of lace, and the train seemed to stretch for miles. An overlayer of tulle from her veil laid atop it like a cloud.

This woman was the closest thing he'd ever seen to an angel on earth, and the flame of the sun only emphasized the stunning scene at the end of the red-carpeted aisle.

Anneliese held her father's hand carefully. The king sat in his wheelchair and was pushed down the aisle by an attendant.

When they came to the end of the aisle, the king reached his hand toward Matt's.

Matt had expected the king's hand to be cold and thin, but instead, he felt a deep warmth. The king joined Anneliese's hand with Matt's and with stilted syllables in a raspy voice addressed his future son-in-law. Matt knew he'd rehearsed with speech therapists just to say whatever he was about to say, and Matt knew the message would be meaningful.

"Go with my blessing, and may you have a lifetime of good together."

Then, he signaled his attendant and was wheeled to his place of honor beside the altar area.

A lifetime of good—Matt tucked those words in his heart.

He ascended the three stairs to the altar, Anneliese's hand tightly in his own. Her serene poise and the careful hint of a smile on her rose-tinted lips steadied him.

As the archbishop of San Petro began the service, he addressed both of them formally. Anneliese's name was long, full of titles and middle names.

She paused before answering the archbishop, and he looked at her with a mild spark of alarm, as though wordlessly asking if he'd gotten her name wrong.

"All that is correct, sir," she said with a smile that matched the illumination from the Port Provident lighthouse they'd once loved to sit under. "But he just calls me Annie."

You Don't Have to Leave Port Provident!
Start *Holiday of Hope* Now!

It's a season for miracles—and Port Provident desperately needs one. The hurricane is gone, but so are the tourists who drive the town's economy. How will Port Provident get the holiday cheer the residents so desperately need? Find out now in the conclusion to the best-selling Port Provident: Hurricane Hope series.

HOLIDAY OF HOPE

SHE WAS LOSING FAITH...UNTIL HE BELIEVED IN HER

For four generations, Bretton's on the Boardwalk, a store dedicated to Christmas, has greeted tourists who come to Port Provident, but after Hurricane Hope tears through town, Jessica Bretton is left with a pile of bills to pay and no tourists visiting her store. She doesn't want to fail her family by closing the doors to the store, but she can't hold on much longer.

As Director of the Park Board of Port Provident, Bradley Thorpe is responsible for getting tourists to Provident Island. It's been almost three months since Hurricane Hope tore through the island, and while there's much work to be done, people are ready to get back to normal. The local economy is strained and it looks like the Christmas season is going to be an unhappy holiday.

When Jessica suggests reviving a Christmas celebration from Port Provident's history books, Bradley is unconvinced. His role is to drive the local economy, not plan parties. Could a woman who celebrates

Christmas all year long change the heart of a man who's more interested in the bottom line than a season of hope? And could a little Christmas cheer be just what Port Provident needs to rebuild?

WANT MORE OF PORT PROVIDENT?

Would you like a reader-exclusive free Port Provident story?
Join my reader society today and get A Place to Find Love, a sweet
escape Port Provident romance, available only for newsletter
subscribers!
https://www.subscribepage.com/kristenethridgenewsletter

CAN I ASK YOU FOR A SMALL FAVOR?

If you liked this story, I'd like to ask you to please leave a review. Help me spread the word about Port Provident on Amazon. Most major retailers depend on an algorithm to boost a book's visibility among readers browsing for new titles. Reviews play a major role in how those algorithms work.

I'd appreciate your help in letting other readers just like you know about *His Texas Princess's* hope, heart, and happily-ever-after. It's not about the length of the review—even just a few words like "Good story —I enjoyed it" may seem simple, but can help other readers like you know this is a story worth picking up.

PORT PROVIDENT: HURRICANE HOPE SERIES

Read the Entire Port Provident: Hurricane Hope Series

Shelter from the Storm
The Doctor's Unexpected Family
His Texas Princess
Holiday of Hope

Love Hallmark movies? Pick up Kristen's book October Kiss, based on
the Hallmark movie viewers love! Available anywhere books are sold
—in paperback, digital, and audio!
October Kiss from Hallmark Publishing

ABOUT KRISTEN

Kristen Ethridge writes Sweet Escape Romance—stories with hope, heart and happily-ever-after—for Harlequin's Love Inspired line, Hallmark Publishing, and Laurel Lock Publishing. She's a Romance Writers of America Golden Heart Award nominee and both an Amazon Christian Fiction and Inspirational Romance #1 Best-Selling Author.

You can find Kristen in her native habitat—a Texas patio—where she's likely to be savoring the joy of a crispy taco, along with a glass of iced tea. Scents from her essential oil diffuser are also a must, since she's a certified aromatherapist. She's almost convinced her family that it's normal to talk to imaginary people, as long it goes in a book.

Find her online at http://www.kristenethridge.com and on Amazon and Bookbub. You can get a free story for signing up for her newsletter at https://www.subscribepage.com/kristenethridgenewsletter. You can also follow her adventures in writing at www.facebook.com/kristenethridgebooks.

www.kristenethridge.com
https://www.facebook.com/KristenEthridgeBooks
https://instagram.com/kristenethridge

Don't forget…if you love sweet escape romances, join Kristen's newsletter!

ACKNOWLEDGMENTS

Once again, the events in this book were inspired by my own experiences recovering from 2008's Hurricane Ike in Galveston, Texas. So many people came out to help people they didn't even know. For all of you who volunteer with relief organizations or support them monetarily, I thank you. This book is for you. You've helped carry the load for someone whose shoulders are very weary at a tough time in their lives.

And as always, to my wonderful family: Brian, Carrie and Linnie and Bennett. Thanks for not questioning why I sit in a chair a lot. It's so much easier to do this with a supportive team, and I don't know of one better than Team Ethridge.

∾

"When you pass through the waters, I will be with you…"
—ISAIAH 43:2

∾